OFF-WORLDERS

By

SS DELAUNAY

Thank you

Thank you to everyone, ever, who cheered for
creativity over conformity, power over subservience and
freedom over fear. You are the true world shapers and the
bringers of magnificent things.

Dedicated to

Dedicated to you, dear reader. You honor me in
letting me share my stories with you.

Off-Worlders - Table of Contents

Outpost

Red6 surveyed the monochrome wasteland before him with a distaste bordering on hatred. Not bordering. He did hate it. He fucking hated it.

"I hate this place."

Blue8 snorted in his attempt to suppress a laugh. Red6 made this observation several times a day and it never ceased to amuse Blue8. Of course, Blue8 had spent the last 29 years listening to new recruits express similar sentiments on their first tour of duty in the salt plains.

Blues were few. So Blue8 was literally the 8th Blue to be stationed at this outpost station. Reds, on the other hand were comparatively numerous. It was good that when they got to Red99, they simply started at Red1 again. Otherwise this Red would have a five-digit number assigned to him. Just 6 was better. Much better. Especially for Blue8, who would have had to remember it.

"Secure that scope and prepare to bunker down," Blue8 ordered Red6, his dark silver eyes scanning the horizon with a practiced gaze. "This one's going to be a beauty."

Red6 swore steadily under his breath as he went about his task. Blue8 smiled to himself and headed into the outer hub.

Two terrain vehicles, Desert1 and Desert2, stood side by side. Desert2 had a bobbing yoda on its dash. Blue8 had no idea what a yoda was. It had been a gift from one of the Sprites he had regular dealings with. But he liked the little fella sitting on the dash of the vehicle. He had a fine set of ears and a reassuring air to him.

The Sprite had remarked the yoda would look better on the sputnik. But Blue8 liked him on the terrain vehicle. Besides, the sputnik was weird enough all on its own. He sighed as he looked at it while he waited for the scanner to read his pineal signature. It took up way too much space, that sputnik, and Blue8 disliked having things about that were no clear use to them.

And a broken, bejeweled, Cirillean planetary transitioner was definitely no use to them.

But he had strict orders from his Federation superiors. The thing was worth a fortune. They must keep it there and guard it, until they sent a ship big enough to collect it.

That had been how long ago now? Years? Tens of years?

Blue8 grunted and moved inside.

Blue8's own first tour of duty here had come to an abrupt end when he'd disobeyed a direct order not to offload a written-off terrain vehicle to the Sprite who gave him the yoda.

"Do not give the Sprites anything. Do not talk to the Sprites. Do not engage with them, period," he was warned when he returned, the yoda safely tucked away in his pack.

He had a regular woman and two young children by then, but he'd still jumped at the chance to come back here. The regular woman had long since moved on and his children barely knew him, or he them.

He had never gone back. He'd stayed here. He'd served well. And the Reds they gave him to train up over the years had been children enough for him.

As for the Sprites, well he was more circumspect in his dealings with them, and knew better how to keep a secret.

It was a short walk down a well-lit corridor to their quarters proper. Eerily quiet now after the noise outside of the oncoming storm.

A wall blazed with the incongruent images of mute feeds deemed necessary by The Federation. There should have been sound on at least one of them. But Blue8 had tired of those in love with the sound of their own voices long ago. He shook his head. Bad management everywhere. They were always the ones convinced everyone else wanted to listen to further evidence of their rambling incompetence.

Most of them would be better served just shutting it. But hey, if they weren't going to, he was happy to do it for them.

If he could have turned off the feeds completely he would have done that too. He would have been more than content with the real images of this place. But that was beyond his control so Blue8 simply ignored them as best he could.

What he didn't ignore entirely was the desert scanner.

There were many things in these salt plains, and in the rock mountains beyond them, who could at any time decide to pay them a visit. There had been some unfortunate visits over the years the Federation had a base here, and many wild tales abounded. When Blue8 had first been stationed here, he had been glued to it, whenever he had been confined to being inside.

But there had been no visits and no movement on the radar towards them for several years now.

So, of late, although he didn't ignore it completely, his regulation glances had been cursory at best.

Red6 was more fascinated with it and more disciplined. He was a good lad. Blue8 thought he'd make a fine officer one day. But he was young enough still to be coltish and distracted easily. Young enough to lose his calm and his focus.

"I fucking wish something would show up on this. I fucking wish something would happen!" Red6 had gotten frustrated after his first weeks adjusting to life at the outpost.

Blue8 smiled.

"Don't you?" he demanded of Blue8.

"I don't know," Blue8 replied thoughtfully. "But if something does show up on there, I'd prefer it to be a different something than the something that separated Blue7's head from his shoulders."

Red6 blanched, visibly, and Blue8 took pity on him. "Hey, by all accounts the one Blue1 picked up was a real peach."

Red6 looked unconvinced. "Blue1? You mean like the original Blue1 stationed here? That was like over 1000 years ago. What have they been like since then?"

"Hmmm," Blue8 considered his question carefully. "Generally speaking, not so peachy."

Red6 was beginning to look a little wild eyed and Blue8 laid a steadying hand on his shoulder. "Calm down Red6. It's going to be all right. Remember, we're not here to catch desert monsters, we're here to catch Sirens."

Red6 calmed a little and then said sulkily, "But we won't even get to see her, will we? All we'll get is some signal that she's risen."

Blue8 laughed. "That'll be some signal to bear witness to. The Veil Sirens rise once in an age. There's only been four in existence that we know of before this one."

Red6 sighed, "I know. It would just be cool to see her for real, is all. They're smoking hot, you know."

Blue8 smiled, "They're Sirens. I think it sort of comes with the territory."

Red6 scuffed at the floor with his boot. "Do you believe what they say about them? That they sing you your freedom song? That they set you free from…," he gestured around him, "this?"

Blue8's eyes followed his gesture, "It'd be nice. But who's to know for certain?"

Life at the base had gone on. No desert monsters on the scanner, and no Sirens rising.

Blue8 turned away from the scanner and began to make preparations for dinner.

Food and a good long sleep. The only things these sandstorms were good for.

The bots could watch over the station. There was nothing so crude and primitive as the need for sleep on their agenda.

Blue8 and Red6 slept.

The sandstorm raged outside.

One of the bots completed his customary sweep of the station and came to check the scanner.

On the scanner, in the midst of the sand storm, a little red blip moved inexorably towards them.

The bot registered that it was impossible for anything to be moving about in the sandstorm, let alone moving towards them with such perfect direction. But here it was, anyway.

The bot sequenced to raise the alarm, and failed.

The second bot, sensing the unusual and unexpected deactivation of the first, moved to the scanner.

The little red blip on the scanner had made good ground.

The second bot sequenced to raise the alarm, and failed.

Blue8 and Red6 slept. And the sandstorm raged outside.

In-fact, the desert winds beat relentlessly against their snug little home for some 3 more hours.

At 0500 the main hub alarm and each of Blue8's and Red6's individual alarms failed to activate. Remained silent.

Neither bot had come back online.

Which was odd indeed. Because the bots and the alarms were the best the Federation could supply. For even one of these regularly maintained alarms and two bots to fail would have been unlikely. For all five to fail, highly unlikely indeed.

And verging on the realm of the impossible, which is always an area difficult to deal with. No matter how many times a day the realm of the impossible has the audacity to reveal itself.

And as Blue8 and Red6 slumbered deeply on past 0600, the sandstorm passed over them and silence fell over the plain.

"RREEEEEEEEEEEEEEHHHHHHHHHHHH!!!!!!!!!!!!!"

"RREEEEEEEEEEEEEEHHHHHHHHHHHH!!!!!!!!!!!!!"

"RREEEEEEEEEEEEEEHHHHHHHHHHHH!!!!!!!!!!!!!"

"What the hell!" Blue8 was awake and on his feet in an instant. He was already punching commands into the screen of the main console when Red6 appeared.

Mercifully, the screeching ceased.

"Get those bots back up, Red6!" Blue8 ordered, when he looked up to see Red6 still at the scanner.

"Ah Sir, I think you're gonna wanna come see this," Red6 replied. "There's something out there!"

"What?"

"The scanner. Look. There's something out there!"

"Fark!" Blue8 swore. "That's not out, that's in. Guns, now!"

The little red blip began moving unnaturally fast toward them.

The bashing on the inner airtight doors was so loud it shook the station.

"Max stun," Blue8 barked at Red6 as they took the corridor at maximum speed. It was a strict Federation order on outposts such as these. Where the host planets did not want them there and tolerated them only under strict conditions. One of which was not killing the locals, unless absolutely necessary. Even then, you had better pray your definition of necessary matched the powers and politics that be.

The Federation, like most successful, long term ruling bodies, maintained Cosmic order on the *threat* of force, rather than the actual use of it. Once you started to use force and others retaliated in kind, it all got rather messy, rather quickly.

Having said that, when the Federation did use force, it was brutal, far-reaching and effective.

It was good that it was rare.

Blue8 noticed the small adjustment Red6 made to his blaster out of the corner of his eye and was glad he had reminded the young one. It was a strict Federation order that could easily get forgotten in the heat of the moment. And one that could have massive consequences if the wrong local was taken out. Particularly on a world belonging to the Old Ones.

Red6 rolled neatly into position on the opposite side of the doors.

There was nothing in the room. The airtight doors were shut tight. Whatever had knocked at them had knocked loudly enough to wake the dead, but it was still outside. Not as outside as Red6 would have liked it to be. It had breached the outer hub. But he'd take it.

Blue8 kept his gun steady on the doors. It was like a mini red sandstorm was happening behind the window glass. He couldn't see a thing except for swirling red dust.

Slowly, the dust settled and two words began to emerge. They were two words advised to each Blue who served here. They were not words communicated to or known by the Reds who served with them.

Which was ironic in a way, because, as was customary, the words were always written in red.

Blue8 spoke quietly. "Set to kill," he said to Red6. "Set to kill - Elemental-1."

Red6 swallowed hard, but quickly adjusted his gun without faltering its aim or moving his eyes from the pane of bullet proof glass. The blood was beginning to run down it, rendering the mysterious words unreadable. The dust was almost dissipated. He could see nothing out there. Elemental. A fucking Elemental had attacked them!

"RREEEEEEEEEEEEEEHHHHHHHHHHHHH!!!!!!!!!!!!
"

"RREEEEEEEEEEEEEEEHHHHHHHHHHHHHH!!!!!!!!!
!!!!"

"RREEEEEEEEEEEEEEEHHHHHHHHHHHHHH!!!!!!!!!
!!!!"

"Fark!" They cursed in unison. The motion detector
between the doors quieted quickly again.

" Sir! It's inside the airlock!" Red6's voice was a little
ragged.

"No. It was inside the airlock but it's out," Blue8 was
already at the door. Red6 hadn't even seen him move and
it startled him.

This Blue was so grounded and straight down the
line, it was easy to forget the magic that coursed through
his veins. That the Blues were the elite mage military of
the Federation. The closest thing they would ever have in
power, to the Echelon of the Old Ones. Possessing levels
of ability above and beyond the Reds, who held their own
well enough in the more esoteric units of the armed
forces, but still.

Red6 felt the Blue's eyes on him and he brought his
mind back to the job.

Blue8 signaled the countdown and the offensive silently with his fingers and hit the release.

The door hissed open, the dripping blood markings on the small glass panel disappearing into the wall.

Blue8 moved through low, while Red6 covered him in a hail of elemental taking out capable laser, that cost more to produce than two years of his wages.

Once Blue8 was safely ensconced behind the terrain vehicle, Desert1, he returned the favor to Red6 who bunkered in behind Desert2.

This was going to be an expensive day for the powers that be, Blue8 thought absently to himself as he noticed the softly glowing light on the yoda on Desert2. The thing had a light? Funny, he'd never noticed it before.

A blast of silver laser shot close by his head, bringing his mind back to the present.

Silver laser?

That was a Pirate weapon, not an Elemental attack.

But what the fark were Pirates doing with an Elemental?

They weren't. They couldn't be. The Elementals didn't discriminate amongst human forms. They hated all of them pretty much equally and killed the same.

The Elemental was gone, or far enough away, for the Pirates to take their chances in the wake of its carnage.

But how did Pirates get on an Old Ones' world? How did they even know this base was here?

Blue8 signaled Red6. "Switch to standard human kill," he commanded. No point wasting Elemental-1 on these bastards. But the Pirates wouldn't hesitate to kill them, they were not locals and the Federation was always happy about dead Pirates. No sense wasting stun.

"Oh, but you insult me, Federation agent," the tone was mocking, the accent heavy. "I assure you, we are far from standard."

"Good for you," Blue8 replied, when the next barrage of silver laser was over. "But my gun will just do you as standard all the same."

There was a bark of laughter. "That is no way for the Federation to speak to its loyal citizens."

"Loyal Federation citizens don't storm its bases and terrorize and steal from its other citizens for their criminal livelihoods," Blue8 retorted. He was listening to movement, factoring where the leader's voice was coming from, as opposed to where he was projecting it - an old Pirate trick - and getting a gage on numbers.

He dove quickly to the other end of the terrain vehicle and fired off a round over its rear. He dropped two of them, there were still at least five more plus the leader.

"But we didn't storm your base," the Pirate gasped in mock indignation, and giving no indication that the downed men meant anything to him. "The Elemental did that more than adequately. They don't like you here you know. Those words on the door in that poor Sprite's blood. Tsch. Tsch." There was a slight pause and Blue8 tracked his almost imperceptible movement with his gun. When the Pirate spoke again, his voice was exactly where Blue8 was aiming.

Blue8 smiled to himself and Red6 looked impressed, and a little more sure of himself.

"Do you know what those words mean, little red experiment?" the Pirate leader drawled casually. "Do you know what the Elemental has cursed you with?"

Red6 responded by firing off a round of his own, and then dropping quickly back down again, as a streak of silver damage came by way too close for comfort.

"You should stop now," Blue8 called, at the same time as giving a series of hand signals to Red6. "You have no idea what you're talking about."

"Aim down slightly," he ordered Blue8 quietly. "You need to factor in the up-take."

Red6 nodded fervently and waited for Blue8's next signal.

Blue8 was aware the Pirates were stalling, firing off only routine rounds in their general direction to keep them bunkered down behind the terrain vehicles. They were up to something and they needed to get on the offensive with them STAT.

"Oh, but I do, Blue8, I do," the Pirate drawled on. "I have very much an idea of what I am talking about."

The sound of a voice speaking in a language neither Blue8 or Red6 understood, broke quietly but urgently, over the Pirate's comms.

"Ah, and it seems your little friend returns," the Pirate's voice was not so casual now. "We will just take what is ours and leave you to entertain the Elemental."

Blue8 and Red6 exploded simultaneously above the lower front end of their respective terrain vehicles, guns blazing.

Blue8 was rewarded with a grunt of pain and a spreading patch of red blood on the shoulder of the Pirate leader. But he moved well enough and was secure in his own armored vehicle before they could do any further damage.

The vehicle was huge and it was carrying a rather large payload as it sped through a gaping hole in the wall of the outer hub.

"Motherfucker!" Red6 gasped. "They've got sputnik!"

"Dammit!" Blue8 cursed. He made incredibly fast - too fast - adjustments on his blaster and launched a volley of ridiculous blasts after the vehicle.

Red6 looked on, and then down at his own gun, fairly confident his regulation Federation blaster had no such options available on *it*.

No matter. The vehicle was well equipped to withstand what Blue8 had unleashed on it, and it was fast. And already, almost long gone, a swirl of desert sand camouflaging it nicely. Their ship must be nearby, though, Blue8 thought. Even with something that sophisticated, they would not want to be long in the desert with an Elemental still potentially about.

"Dammit!" he cursed again. Expensive day at the office indeed. There was going to be hell to pay over this. But what could they do? There had been nothing to indicate the Pirates had been watching or tracking them.

And the holes the Elemental had ripped in the outer hub? He'd never seen anything like it.

And if they'd really wanted the sputnik that badly, they should have picked it up years ago instead of leaving it here.

Blue8 sniffed the air. There was the smell of sulphur on it. His skin prickled and a sense of dread hit him in the gut. The Elemental was on its way back again.

"Get inside. Now!" he barked at Red6.

The young soldier didn't need to be told twice.

Blue8 glanced around him. What to take in with them? Nothing. It was all too big. It was why they left it out here in the first place. He slammed his fist down on Desert1 in frustration and prayed the creature would leave them at least one Terrain Vehicle in-tact when it was through with them.

When it was through with them, would they even need a Terrain Vehicle? He pushed the thought from his mind and grabbed the yoda. Damned if the Elemental was getting that.

He secured both airtight doors. The window on the inner one bore the streaks of red blood and red dust.

There was another door off the foyer into the corridor, thick and titanium, which could be dropped down and locked into place. Only in an extreme emergency. Blue8 was confidant this qualified.

He dropped it and locked it and went to join Red6.

"What do we do?" Red6 demanded of him again, as he emerged from the corridor. "How are we supposed to deal with this?"

"We do as we've been ordered," Blue8 replied. "We follow procedure."

"You've dropped the door," Red6 said.

Blue8 laid a steadying hand on his shoulder. "Yeah, I've dropped the door." He turned and placed the yoda on the desert scanner. "Why don't you see if you can get those bots working? Get some of these systems back on line."

There was a lot to do. A lot to repair, even in here. That was good. It would keep them busy.

"But what if…?"

"What if nothing," Blue8 cut him off. "We do as we've been ordered. Get those bots working."

Red6 let out a deep breath and went to work.

Blue8 got one of the outer alarm systems back up in short order. He kept to himself that the Pirates had seemingly helped themselves to all of the outer mounted guns. The kid was already freaking out. No need to scare him further.

The men worked in silence for a time, focused and intent on their tasks.

"I can't get these bots back up," Red6 stood up away from the one he was working on in disgust.

"That's Ok, son," Blue8's voice was quiet and distant.

Red6 looked up, concerned. Blue8 had never called him that. Blue8 was looking at the scanner.

"It's back," Red6 whispered.

"It's back," Blue8 nodded. "Guns. Set to kill. Elemental-1."

"But it can't get through the door," Red6 said as he moved to stand beside Blue8 and watched the red blip move steadily across the desert towards them.

"Guns, Red6," Blue8 repeated.

Red6 got the guns. They were freshly charged and loaded. They had more. They had plenty of guns. Guns were not the problem.

They sat and waited. The red blip gained speed and ground towards them.

"How does it gain speed like that?" Red6 asked.

"Fresh kills," Blue8 replied. "Human, animal, environment, the elements. Whatever can give it what it needs, it will take from."

"What did the Pirate mean?" Red6 pressed on. "When he said it had cursed me? And why did he call me an experiment?"

Blue8 sighed heavily. "Don't listen to Pirates, Red6. They spread nothing but stuff and nonsense."

"It wrote words on the door, in the glass on the door, in blood!" Red6's voice was raising in volume. "You know what they mean, you know you do!" His voice was very loud and accusing now, the blaster he clutched waived unsteadily in his hands.

"Easy, Red6," Blue8 looked at him sharply. "Those words are classified."

He held up a hand before Red6 could speak again. "And nothing to do with you."

Blue8 cast his dark silver eyes back to the scanner quickly. It was a lie, but it was a lie Red6 needed to believe right now, if he was to have any hope of getting through this.

"Dammit," this time the curse was quiet and resigned. "It's here."

Red6 started and glanced at the scanner. The red blip was still, dead.

The pounding on the titanium door was ridiculous.

"Oh, my godds, it's already in," Red6 gasped.

He said it to air. Blue8 was already down the corridor, taking position, gun aimed, in front of the door.

Red6 paled when he joined him and saw the dents the thing had already made in impenetrable titanium steel.

In the main control room, the yoda started to glow.

And one of the bots slowly reactivated.

*****

The Sprite who had given the yoda to Blue8 came to in his chains and cursed. He could sense the movement and intent of the Elemental.

The fool, the Sprite thought to himself with genuine affection. He liked Blue8. The Blue did not know his true power, his true value. None of the Blues did. The Federation harnessed them carefully like that. He hoped this Blue would know it and know it soon. He deserved as much. The Sprite sighed. He had done his best and told him to move the yoda to the "sputnik."

The pattern the Pann Lords had seen and shown to the Sprite ran deep. The Siren would need the Cirillean sputnik, and the Pirates. The Pann Lords knew this, as did the Sprites. And it seemed, so did this Elemental.

And this Elemental was an Elemental of the Old Ones and must be stopped.

If they had left the yoda on the sputnik, the Elemental would not have been able to follow it off-world with the Pirates, and perhaps, would have left them alone.

But no mind. The Fifth Siren of the Veil was soon to rise, and he had done his bit. After all these years, the Cirillean transitioner and the Pirates were launched into play.

The fool, the Sprite thought to himself again, as the Old Ones' Echelon guard approached, and he mercifully lost consciousness again. He must have taken it inside, was the last thought he remembered thinking.

*****

The bot reactivated his droid companion and signaled command central once again for assistance.

The bot was sad he had missed Blue8's departure. The bot had been here a long time and Blue8 had been his favorite.

The most powerful of all the Blues and the most grounded. Decent. He was a decent sentient being. The bot was an older model and had served other places before this one. Enough to know that this was not the norm, as sentient beings liked to tell themselves, but a rarity.

Still, it was unclear to the bot why the Federation treated the Blues as they did. Why they harnessed them in such a way they would never know who they truly were, and how powerful. Surely, they would be more value to the Federation *in* their full power?

As he watched the Federation ship depart, he laid his Cytech hand over the feed. "Goddspeed, Blue8. Goddspeed."

He felt only a small pang for Red6, but he had not known the young soldier long, and it took time for bots to develop feelings for other beings.

Still, he had cleaned what remained of the young Red with care from the floor and walls. The Elemental creature had not left much. Not physical anyway. The biggest bit, the invisible bit of Red6, it had consumed and taken with it.

The Old Ones' Elementals here hungered for the Reds, in a way they did not hunger for the Blues.

Perhaps because the Blues had better shields over that part of themselves, and it could not be taken from them quite so easily.

It was something to ponder while they waited for central command to collect them. It was still unclear and confusing to the bot why they had not been taken on the first ship with the selected equipment, and the remains - far more intact than those of Red6 - of Blue8.

"Goodbye, Blue8," the bot said again and moved away from the feed, his farewell to the longest serving Blue at the outpost complete.

And Blue8, wherever he was, and he was many places all at once now, felt it. He did not know what had happened. But he felt something like a small string cut loose. And it made him crazy. It made him careen through the desert even more wildly. It surged through him this small action, setting him finally free.

He howled like a wild thing.

It felt good. It felt damn good.

The surreal desert scape before him changed to stars, and he saw the Blue Star, the star of the Siren, rising before him.

And he wondered, as do all those who realize they actually do have a choice, what the hell had taken him so long.

And then it struck him, that perhaps this would have been richer, if he had simply started with this.

With his own path, his own tribe to hurtle towards, and his own rebel yell ringing out across desert sands and cosmic skies.

But then again, maybe not.

Maybe it was the contrast that made the blood surge in his veins, and brought the first tears of his life to his eyes.

Blue8 howled like a wild thing again.

And did not care.

And the Sprite smiled.

Queen

Evamiin waited to be called.

There had been few instances in her life that Evamiin had waited to be called for anything.

But the call to the Third Tower of Aakbiishen was one she heeded, however reluctantly, and however she thought at times she may not.

There are three towers of Aakbiishen but only two are visible to you if you have not been initiated by the Pann.

The great irony being that Evamiin had been initiated by them. But the vision required to see the third tower had never opened to her.

It happens sometimes, they had said. And said no more. It was the end of it.

At first it had driven her mad. Eaten away at her. But they called her here rarely enough now.

They had ceased calling her here regularly, after the first time she had moved against them, without their knowledge.

So long ago. But unforgivable even now, it seemed.

Memories. As she looked down on the world she ruled - for she did still rule here - memories flooded her.

It was another reason she did not like coming here. They always made her wait. Gave her too much time to remember. Too much time to think.

But there was always the possibility that he would be here. And so, in the end, despite her deep misgivings, she always came.

His horns were white obsidian now. They had been black when they'd first met. Still, the rainbow colors of the cosmos swirled within. Lit by spirit fire. Lit by ancient memory, ancient flame.

They had come here knowing nothing, her family, nothing.

Only that a portal was here. An inverse portal to the Other Cosmos. And to which they had the key.

They had the crystal.

Not the rare, natural, inverse portal crystals of the Sirens or the Ancient Giant Astronauts, but the closet approximation to it. Wrought by her father's finest bio-engineers over the course of not years, but decades.

They were sure it would work.

They just needed a world with an inverse portal to test it on.

And what better, than this jewel of a world, Moethiica. Seemingly untamable. A history of legend and superstition surrounding it. How it rid itself of all who tried to conquer it by simply rotting from within. Destroying. Rendering itself dead, poisonous, uninhabitable.

And then thriving again, once it's would be usurpers and inhabiters had left.

They were about to become the most powerful Old Family in The Federation. They would take Moethiica and its inverse portal for their own.

Her father knew The Federation wanted it. Evamiin did not know how he knew such a thing, but he did.

She remembered the excitement she'd felt as they built their life here on this mysterious, beautiful and intoxicating world. Her love was the most promising young leader in her father's Militia. She had no doubt he would ask to marry her.

She had no doubt she would say yes.

She was walking in the long-overgrown gardens idly planning her wedding. They had built a home in the ancient ruins on the eastern side of The Forest. Her father planned to restore the ruins to their former glory. Their new home, their new palace, would be here. In the heart of The Forest. Close to the portal.

He scoffed at the warnings of the local population of Ibecca, the crude, backwater town which stood even then as the main and only city of Moethiica. They had begged them not to enter The Forest. To leave The Forest and the portal be.

And now here they were. Poised to take it. Poised to open the gateway to the Other Cosmos. Poised to be powerful and wealthy beyond all their imagining.

They were the almost embarrassing, poorer relations to many amongst the Old Ones. She could not wait to have those vile snobs who had ostracized her and laughed at her, toady to her once her father and his Militia were done.

She stopped near an exquisite old fountain, long out of use. Fashioned by one of Moethiica's previous would be conquerors. Home now to worms instead of fish. Creeping vines and dirt instead of water.

It was a favorite place. They had met here last night when she crept undetected from her room. She ran her fingers along the place on the fountain's edge where he had held her. She remembered exquisite kisses. She remembered his hands on her, his body pressed hard against hers, pushing her back against the cold, hard stone.

His kisses had grown rougher, more insistent, more urgent. She had felt his breathing change. When she placed two hands on his chest and pushed him back from her, she heard him groan.

He had not been happy but he had let her go. He had no choice. She was her father's daughter.

"Evamiin!" It was her mother calling her. Communicators sometimes disguised emotions. But there was a slight edge to her mother's voice that perhaps only a daughter could hear. "Evamiin! Evamiin!" There was more urgency now.

A breeze rustled suddenly through the stillness. A twig snapped loudly underfoot.

She felt a chill run through her like ice.

Something touched the back of her head. Like a whisper.

She did not look up to meet the eyes she suddenly felt upon her.

She ran. She ran and she did not look back.

And the chill wind ran with her, whispering. Whispering, laughing, mocking. A constant stream of chill murmurings in her head.

She stumbled and fell, cutting her hand sharply on a jagged rock as she rose.

She pushed the bloodied hand against her waist to stem the bleeding. Rich blue blood mixed with chocolate earth, and the emerald leaves of the forest floor, now caked against her.

She made it home.

The huge front doors stood open. Her mother stood between them, two House Militia at her side. She was so pale she was white. She wrung her hands until Evamiin was through the opening, and then the Militia slammed the doors closed.

Evamiin clasped her mother's arms, steadying her, yielding answers from her sobs.

Sirens.

There had been a nest of them guarding the portal. The men had not stood a chance.

It was her love they had let return to tell the story. Evamiin sat with him during his last moments. His wounds bleeding out, his eyes glazed over, he grasped her hand not knowing who she was. A man possessed. They had massacred the Militia. Killed her father and brothers, his friends.

But all he could talk about was their magnificence. All he could hear was their song.

"The Siren," he whispered to her. His eyes wide, his entire body and voice enthralled. He had never felt such love, such warmth, never seen such exquisite beauty. He sighed, looking truly blissful, truly at peace. It was a freedom song, he said, before he closed his eyes and let them take him. He had smiled at her. He seemed happy to be going.

And then he too, was gone.

Evamiin sat in silence, his cold hand in hers. She did not cry. She did not try to make sense of his words. Because she could not make sense of them.

There was another Evamiin who had existed before this day, who perhaps could have made sense of them, but that Evamiin could not hold on. That Evamiin was slipping away. She could feel her slipping.

How long had she sat like this?

When did she go?

There was chaos, madness all around her.

"Excuse me, My Lady Evamiin." It was one of the House Militia. He kneeled down low beside her, speaking to her gently. "Excuse me My Lady, but we are evacuating. We must move out now. Your mother is sedated and we have her on a transport. We will move his body for you. We fear they are massing to strike again. We need to get you on the transport now."

His body. She looked at the Guard with vacant eyes. His hand was so cold now. So cold and so rigid in her tight hand. She could not let go. And she could not look at him. But even as she thought it, her eyes moved involuntarily towards his face.

And stopped before they reached it.

"There is something glowing in his pocket."

As she withdrew it and held it high to the light she could not believe it.

It was the crystal.

Her father had shown it to her only once. But once was enough. One did not forget a would-be inverse portal crystal easily.

It brought the life back in to her. Inspired her to move.

She was her father's daughter. She would finish what he could not.

She clenched the crystal so tight, blue blood welled in her palm.

One of the older Militia laid a steadying hand on her arm.

She looked up at him, startled. Her palm smarted where the skin had broken. She looked down at it in a daze, her fingers slowly uncurling from around the large gemstone.

She shook her head and moved herself to action. She secured the crystal deep in an inner pocket in the belt at her waist.

The remaining Militia assigned just to her, stood at the grand house doors, waiting for her.

The attack was decimating and silent. They had not revealed themselves before she made her exit. They had been waiting for her.

Such weaponry. She had never seen the likes of it before this.

The Forest People, the Silff, said nothing. Just held them in a tight circle. Whatever signals they passed to bring them were undetectable.

There were two of them. They landed simultaneously. When one of them placed her exquisite hand beneath her chin, and lifted her eyes to hers, Evamiin had never felt such a pull to another being, never felt such power.

In the Siren's glorious eyes, she saw galaxies shifting and worlds forming. She heard a song. What a song. The terror became too much for her. Evamiin lost control and wet herself.

The creature smiled.

And then it moved too quickly for her.

It ripped open the inner pocket of her belt containing the crystal with one long dark fingernail like it was made of nothing. It had the crystal. It hurled it to the ground.

At first it sat there between them, unmoving on the forest floor.

And then one key, crucial part of it, splintered.

"Noooooooo!" Screamed Evamiin, and lunged for it.

But the Siren was airborne with the largest piece of it before her cry even ended. When Evamiin jumped, she grabbed at empty air.

And then she realized too late the other Siren had the other splinter.

It was a sharp, thin, pointed shard. As the Siren sank it deep into Evamiin's chest, she smelt honeysuckle. She saw indigo.

She lapsed into coma.

And the glowing crystal shard in her chest became dull, black rock. No longer glowing. Dead.

Nine days she stayed like this. Her mother, hysterical, or sedated, by her side.

The Militia stood guard. Secured lodgings.

One of the Housekeep who had grown familiar with two of the guards, timidly suggested Sprite magic to the nicer of them.

Her timidity was an act, one she had learned useful in survival amongst Moethiica's long line of would be male conquerors.

In truth she preferred the Militia who favored her with attentions that were not so nice. But she sensed that deep down he cared not if the daughter lived or died. To be perfectly honest, neither did she. The girl seemed naught but a bitch if truth be told. She had attended the family briefly in the city when they first arrived here, and had no good memories of her.

But she liked her mother, who she cared for, and felt sorry for the older woman in her grief. She had lost everything. Well, almost everything. The bitch daughter would make it everything. But that's the way life goes sometimes. We get left with those not of our first choosing.

And so, she offered the only thing she had which she thought could help the situation to the one most likely to act on it. And he did. The Sprite was called forth from Junar, the sacred mountain, and the administrations began.

Evamiin was saved. But her perfection was ever marred by a blood scar, blue in her case, where the shard was pulled from.

After sufficient numbers of the Militia sent back into The Forest - the nicer one who had sought the Sprite, among them - were returned in pieces, Evamiin abandoned all attempts to re-enter it.

Without the inverse portal crystal, it was probably useless anyway.

And besides, the crude town of Ibecca was ripe for the taking. Evamiin contented herself with that for a time.

Absently, she ran a finger along the still sharp edge of the blackened shard. She had fashioned it on a chain and had worn it to this day. Remembering.

She had used it in her first kill.

It is a curse to kill a winged, the locals told her.

Evamiin killed one anyway. It was not a Siren. She would not actually see a Siren again until the Junar massacre. But it was female. And it was winged. It would do.

She enjoyed the screams of the creature. She enjoyed watching her guards with it.

Her mother died, begging her daughter to let go of her hate.

But she could not. It whispered to her. A constant, cold, murmuring on the wind.

And then he came.

The Pann do not dwell in the city. They dwell in the desert beyond. The desert is deceiving. Red and rocky, its hills are numerous. And its hills hold caves. Labyrinths of caves and tunnels that descend deep, deep into the earth.

And deep in the earth underneath the hot, rocky, red desert there are lakes. Fathomless lakes in underground caverns lit by the stars. Lit by the swirling jewels of the cosmos.

They are underground.

It is a mystery.

The first time he bedded her, she had never experienced anything like it. Never even conceived that such a level of ecstasy was possible.

She was enthralled to him.

And Evamiin, under the Pann Lord's careful influence, began to shift her focus.

And Moethiica became more than healthy and inhabitable.

It became wealthy and powerful.

But still The Forest and the portal eluded her.

Still, those she sent to enter, returned in pieces.

Still, the locals whispered of the old tales, the old legends. How a Siren and an Old One would one-day change everything.

How the true ruler of Moethiica would be Forest born.

Evamiin fumed and lived with it.

She could do no other.

And The Forest stayed silent and lived with its own.

The violet eyes of the Silff were seen rarely enough in Ibecca proper in those days, but when they were it drove Evamiin mad that they should have this audacity to walk among her people there. And that they could cross the threshold into her world, but not she into theirs.

She protected Moethiica from them as best she could. Not how she would have liked. There were limits to what she could do, which if pushed, brought on the rotting of the very world around her.

So, she let them be, unless one crossed her path. And then she tested those limits afresh.

When the Old Ones established her Elite Guard, her Echelon, that would change, they had assured her. She would still not be able to touch them, but they most certainly would.

"How?" she had demanded.

But these were Old Ones' whose magics and mysteries were of the highest ranking among their kind, and they would tell her nothing.

Still, they acknowledged her. And they were coming here.

Wait for them. It was all she could do for now.

And she still had the memories and souvenirs of Junar to comfort her.

Junar. Yes, it had been a disaster. But at least it had brought the she-devils out of hiding.

The blood splatters on the thirty-foot wings encased above her bed were still perfectly preserved. A reminder, that not all of the casualties of the battle from that confounded mountain had been her own forces.

The mutilated wings gave her hope. That one day she would find a way. Federation Law be damned. If she came across a Siren nest she would kill them all. And wear the consequences of her actions later.

Evamiin let the blackened shard fall from her fingers and pressed her hands against the transparent, curved wall.

How grand and large and magnificent now, this city of hers beneath her. And it was hers. Not theirs. Hers.

It was a heady feeling to be up this high above it. To see it as the godds saw it. The walkway she now stood upon was encased in translucent bubble. Dipped in cloud.

She watched as a Cirillean ship descended through the mists, making its way gracefully to the Ibecca Space Port. A graceful race the Cirilleans. It was mirrored in their space craft.

"Lady Evamiin."

Only one could say her name like that and make her heart skip a beat.

And it had been such a long time. Was he here for her? Or for the meeting?

She stayed looking out at Moethiica, not turning to face him. The Cirillean ship landed safely.

"Lady Evamiin. It is time."

Ah, here for the meeting.

She released the breath she had not realized she'd been holding.

And turned to him.

It was such exquisite pain just to look at him.

His eyes were unreadable but he bowed to her, his white obsidian horns glistening magnificently, even in this subdued light.

She bowed her head in return.

And when she was composed enough to raise it, he held the door open for her, his eyes staring off into the distance. And not at her.

She passed by him quickly, and acutely aware of his presence at her back, paused inside the door. He closed it softly and she felt the tingle at the base of her crown as he made connection with her and opened her vision. Opened her awareness. Opened her world.

The small anteroom before her shifted and changed. Another doorway became possible.

Actually, several doorways became possible, but without the required mastery she would only ever see the one.

She chose it and began the ascent to the Third Tower.

The ancient Pann Lord, who had, so long ago now, expertly closed her off from ever seeing the other doorways, spared a passing glance down on to a version of Moethiica she would never know existed. And at the same time, had been instrumental in constructing.

She would bring the Old Ones soon. And then her part in this larger unfolding would almost be complete. The former essence of her fluttered briefly over his heart. The essence that had enraptured him, that stood on the precipice, that could have gone either way.

Either way they could use. Either way they could work with. But only one way could he love. She had chosen the other.

He dismissed the ghost of that other essence with the merest flick of his fingers, and began what was actually a descent, to the Third Tower of Aakbiishen.

Izabel

Izabel watched the Cirillean ship approach through sapphire eyes. They were the same sapphire eyes of the Lady Evamiin. Not just a similar deep, jewel blue, but exactly so. All of the Gen3s had these eyes. The Lady Evamiin had ordered it.

They were made for a blue planet. Earth. Blue Earth. Little Blue. The Cybriids were created for many things, but with this one ultimate goal, this blue jewel of a planet at the far end of the Cosmos, in mind.

It was on this little blue planet that the great Mind Diamond of the Makers lays undetected, still. It was above this little blue planet that the Veil separating this Cosmos from what was beyond, lay, waiting to be opened. It was from this little blue planet that the Fifth Siren of the Veil would rise.

And the war for control of the Veil would start from there.

An important little blue planet, indeed.

It was only fitting, that these most superior of all CyTech creations should have blue eyes in its honor.

But they were not in its honor. Not really. They were more in honor of the Lady Evamiin's ego.

Deep down, Izabel knew this.

Just as she knew she would never go to Little Blue. Never willingly be a part of the Old Ones desire to take it. Never be a part of the Veil War those with power and control in the cosmos waited for.

She had been created by Old Ones, but she was not one of them.

She was of something much older than them, and who, perhaps, had met their fate, in their hands.

Izabel was beginning to be as sure of this, as she was sure she would never go to Little Blue. She had said it out loud once. When she was very young and first told of the mission.

"I will not go there and do that," she said. She was their star pupil, their star creation. The professor who schooled them had looked her in stunned silence.

She had been sent for testing. Back to her maker, Dr. IIz, but he could find nothing wrong with her.

They dismissed it as a glitch. They did a cleanse and reboot. Her Cytech brain, body, flesh were deactivated for these processes, but that other part of her remained conscious. Not the soul fragment they imparted into her at birth, but the other bit, ancient, knowing, bigger than the soul bit, bigger than all of them.

She learnt much about her inner workings while that other awareness remained conscious during these processes. It would serve her most readily later on.

Like now.

She checked her gun was set to maximum stun only. There was still a risk that maximum stun might kill instead of stun. She tried very hard not to think about that. At the end of the day, she could only guarantee her intentions.

Butterflies.

Knowing calm.

She took out the first flight controller without him even becoming aware of her presence. That fact might bring the current trial of Off-World human flight controllers to an abrupt end. But Izabel thought it was doomed to failure anyway.

There were way too many CyTech enhanced beings for emotionally and physically needy O-W human flight controllers to ever be more than a passing fad.

The second flight controller was CyTech. Not Cybriid like herself, but still. Baden. That was his name. Izabel remembered as she pulled the trigger.

She rubbed her upper left arm. He'd put up more of a struggle than the human.

Security Detail were on their way here in numbers. She could see them on the screens. She knew these men and women well.

They had not questioned her arrival on the flight deck.

Izabel was never questioned.

She was The Lady Evamiin's pet WorldCoder. Why would she be?

Calmly, but with a touch more urgency in her step, Izabel released the door lock and stepped from the control room into the hangar.

She shot the two flight attendants, the three ground crew and the two hangar security detail within five-seconds of entering the hangar.

She is a Cybriid.

And she had modified the gun.

She had taken two bullet wounds herself. But she could fix them. They would heal.

The Cirilleans looked at her. They looked at her gun.

They backed away.

Gracefully.

The Cirilleans are always graceful.

"A graceful race."

"Yes. It is reflected in their space craft."

Izabel wondered if anyone ever said anything else about the Cirilleans.

She nodded to them before she boarded the craft.

It was nothing personal.

It was just that the Cirilleans were the only Off-Worlders allowed entry on the world she was going to.

Perhaps it was the grace thing.

If it weren't for this fact, she would have simply stolen one of Moethiica's ships.

Lights flashed on the hangar flight control desk

She had already coded her exit.

The Cirillean ship left the Ibecca Space Port as quickly and gracefully as it had landed. Only a very short time ago.

The Lady Evamiin was already in her meeting.

The Security Detail arrived thirty-three seconds too late to do anything to stop her.

Timing. Izabel thought as she settled back in to the pilot's chair.

Butterflies. Knowing calm. Timing.

That was the third key element, to a good first step, towards doing something crazy good.

*****

WorldCoding is a highly profitable business.

And a heady rush of power affair to boot.

Most worlds however, did it very, very poorly.

Moethiica, however, did not. Because Moethiica had the best World Coders known to the cosmos. Moethiica had Cybriids.

They had come a long way since the disaster of Gen1. Gen1, who had randomly embodied with the lost souls of an ancient, long destroyed, mystery world.

In their brief existence in the Cybriid Gen1 forms, they had spoken of their fluid, floating being. And they had spoken of being drawn inexplicably to the bodies of these newly created Cybriids, with a burning desire to embody in them.

Dr. IIz, their creator, had wanted more for his creations than the usual human soul snippets used in CyTech.

Suffice to say, he got more than he bargained for. Now embodied with the essence of these ancient beings, their size, strength and intelligence was on a par with, and possibly even greater than, the Giant Ancient Astronauts.

They were incarcerated immediately. For their own protection, as well as for the protection of all else, around them.

There were many, however, on Moethiica who feared and obsessed over their existence. Even behind bars, the reality of these new monsters of The Lady ate away at them.

When the inside attack came on Gen1, it was brutal and efficient.

One, however, survived, and escaped in the aftermath.

He was one of the smaller ones, wiry, strong and clever.

He stole aboard a ship.

He coded. He deactivated his tracker. He hid his tracks cleverly.

And after a time, with no sign of his whereabouts on Moethiica or any other likely worlds, they gave up searching for him.

And they tried again with Gen2, and this time they did things a little differently.

With the success of Gen2 and Gen3, Gen1 and its lone survivor were carefully buried deep in hard to find records, and quickly forgotten. But all living things tap into one ancient mind for part of their consciousness, and the Cybriid were no different.

And in the ancient mind the Cybriids shared, the Gen1 Survivor spoke and became legend.

There were twenty-two in Gen1. There were seven hundred in Gen3 - human sized, carefully bred, accepted. And of them, Izabel, brilliant and beautiful, was the best. She served faithfully and brilliantly, for many, many years.

When the powers that be were informed that Izabel had stolen the Cirillean ship, they did not believe it.

*****

Space.

Nothing but space.

For the first time in her already long life, Izabel was alone. Truly alone.

There were no orders to answer, no Webs to code, no systems to plug into.

Well, there was the ship's system, but only her life depended on that. She was no longer plugged in to the fate of worlds.

And she liked it. She rather liked it.

She hoped the beings she had used the stun gun on were Ok. Truly.

Ok. She remembered that discussion with Arii. No matter where you went in the Cosmos people argued about the origins of the word Ok, or their version of it.

There was something about that word.

But words are like that. The spaces in between the words even more so. Structure. Patterns. The keys to meaning.

She wondered what Arii would think of her now and what she had done.

If there was one person she would like to thank for getting her to this position it would be him.

He had arrived on Moethiica with a warrant for her arrest. But he had never arrested her.

Questioned her, tested her and studied her? Yes. Extensively.

But he had never arrested her. Had never taken her with him from Moethiica.

Though she would have gone with him in a heartbeat if he'd asked. She would have gone with him anywhere.

But he had not asked.

And she had remained.

She had remained but she had never been quite the same again. Her sapphire eyes had been opened. And she could not look at her world or those around her in quite the same light.

Aagghh. The second bullet was stuck fast. With one last hard yank she got it out. She had found a basic first aid kit in the tiny bathroom. She cleaned the wound as best she could and stitched the torn Cybriid flesh together crudely, but adequately.

The flesh would scar and she was immensely pleased with that. She had been taking the pep that was increasingly popular among the Cybriid. It rendered their perfectly engineered flesh vulnerable to the markings of life. The souvenirs that you had lived. She wrapped a bandage around her leg and smiled at it. It made her feel human.

As did the pain. They had been programmed for pain since Gen2. To give then empathy.

And this pain she could live with. This pain was scientific, expected, measurable. It was pain that would pass.

It was the unscientific, unexpected, unmeasurable type of human pain that Izabel was not so fond of. The pain that endures.

Like her heart.

When Arii had eventually left Moethiica, Izabel had felt her heart. And she had felt her heart clearly broken.

This is what Arii had done. He had made her feel things.

Like that awful first time she knew she had disappointed him.

He had been questioning her. She had answered. Well, she thought.

He looked at her, the disappointment evident on his face. He put down the instrument he had been cleaning and leaned against the bench, arms folded across his chest, his earnest, intelligent, brown eyes penetrating.

"Izabel, when you WorldCode do you not see the Structures of thought, and how these structures are manipulated to entangle and ensnare people on the Webs?"

"Yes, I do," she replied. "It is... it is crucial to everything we do."

"And do you not see that the same thing must be happening to you?" His voice was gentle but his eyes were intense.

"Yes, but..." she began, but did not know how to continue. How to say to a human that she was above that. That she was created to exist above the crude structures which ensnared them. She had said it before. But she would not say it to him. Not to this one.

He held up a hand, anyway. "There is no but, Izabel. We are all coded to something. We all believe something. And if we were to look at the structure of the belief, as opposed to the belief itself, it would look exactly the same as the belief which believes the opposite of it."

He turned back to the instrument panel and put the last of them away in his bag. "No matter how superior you believe yourself to be."

She had the grace to blush, and he had the grace to keep his back to her until it faded from her perfect Cybriid cheeks.

"It's the age-old dilemma, isn't it? How do you ever arrive at truth when the very way you have been taught to perceive the world around you, is a lie?"

He snapped his bag shut and turned to her, gesturing to her sapphire eyes.

She had fallen in love with him before he finished his last sentence. And perhaps it was that that made her acutely aware of the faint distaste that emanated from him when he looked into her eyes.

He had made no bones about how he felt about The Lady. And they were her eyes. All the eyes of Gen3 created in her image.

"She gave you her eyes Izabel," he said softly. "You cannot change that. But what other ways to view the world has she given you, that you have not even sought to question?"

And with that he had left her.

When Izabel looked in the mirror that night, all cool blonde pale aesthetic, compared to the lush golden ripeness of The Lady, all she could see was her sapphire eyes. Sapphire eyes that Arii found distasteful.

The next morning, she had asked about having her eyes replaced with new ones, different ones. She thought some green ones, or even a nice silver might be nice. She would have loved the gold tinged violet of the Silff, but she knew she could never admit to that.

She wondered how she had come to admit it to herself.

The Lady Evamiin was hysterical at the request and Izabel never spoke of it again.

The remaining time with Arii, she kept her eyes down and averted from him, hoping he would forget who they reminded him of. Hoping if he did not see her eyes, he would see her, see Izabel.

But it was not to be.

"No matter," Izabel whispered softly to herself as she made an exquisitely smooth gateway jump. Perhaps I will get new eyes on a new world.

She was almost there.

Very soon she would be on the world of the lone survivor of the First Gen.

Not all of them heard the voices. But she did. She heard them so clearly, they were more real to her at times than those around her. And his voice was the loudest and strongest of them all.

He still lived. He was still embodied. She was sure of it.

Idly, she wondered what was happening on Moethiica. For there was still a part of Izabel that was sure, that at the end of this little adventure, she would return to The Lady Evamiin's side, be welcomed back with open arms, and all forgiven.

A part of her was not so sure that this was what she wanted.

Fark!

The screech pierced her ear drums as the 3D image materialized before her. The huge clawed hand swiped at her. She ducked just in time and felt the whoosh of air past her head.

It was no longer 3D.

It was in.

It was at least eight feet tall. The stuff of nightmares. Snub nosed, the eyes were black, opaque, red rimmed. They held horrors. And they held focus. And their focus was Izabel. Pale, withered lips drew back on sharp, pointed, teeth. The head was huge. Strands of lank hair hung from the bulging forehead.

Human ears. Human body. Pale skin. Muscles and big bones. Strong. It was clothed in a loose fitting white tunic, tied at the waist with a brown knotted cord. The dirty, yellow claws on its hands and feet were hideous. It had a long string of small, wooden beads around its neck.

Weeza Gremlin.

She had not expected one of them here.

It shrieked again, moving with a speed and agility that belied its size.

When it swiped at her, it opened a nasty gash on her forehead. Izabel cursed, hit the floor and rolled, drawing her gun as she did. She flicked it to kill and fired.

Nothing.

She had entered the inner Web of the world carefully and cleverly coded as a Cirillean. Moethiica's weapons had been rendered useless in the process.

She cursed. She had been too preoccupied with thoughts of Arii to recode the weaponry. She was not normally so careless.

The Weeza Gremlin howled in delight and threw itself upon her. She threw a textbook elbow from the bottom, releasing her needle probe, and impaling the Gremlin's head on it.

She sent the same charge through the needle probe that she would to destroy a very large system.

It had the desired effect.

The Gremlin's head exploded in a pulpous mass all over her.

That bit was not so desired.

She pushed the hideous body off of her and raised herself to her feet, shaking the muck from her as best she could.

Damn it!

The ship had been locked and was being tracked in.

She was in view of them now.

It would seem she had quite a welcoming party.

A heavily armed welcoming party.

Izabel sighed and went to make use of the ship's tiny bathroom.

It was a fairly primitive world. They had actually slowed her descent and would be a while tracking her in.

As she peeled off her ruined clothes and let the steaming hot water wash away gremlin brains and other muck, she wondered what they had done to attract the attention of the Weeza Gremlins.

She shivered, in spite of the heat and the steam.

She would need to take a closer look at their Webs.

*****

When they finally landed her ship, the Weeza Gremlin was beginning to smell.

Badly.

Izabel sighed. She had enjoyed flying this ship. She truly hoped its previous crew were well.

She had expected them to board the ship as soon as she docked. But instead they stayed on the ground, their ancient weaponry leveled at her. A man in uniform used some sort of portable speaker system to command her loudly to exit the ship.

Izabel hesitated. She had amused herself on the way down with overriding the locking code they had placed on the ship's laser system.

With a press of a turquoise button she could annihilate every last one of them in a matter of seconds. Her finger hovered over the button, and then her hand dropped to her side.

That was not the way she wanted to do this.

And so Izabel descended the stairs of her circular, silver ship in the manner of all people willing to negotiate a little on the finer points of their belief system.

That is, she walked with her hands above her head and did her level best to look contrite and non-threatening.

The man in the uniform had a hat. In fact, they all had hats. Hats were rarely seen on Moethiica which Izabel thought was a great pity. At some stage, she did not remember when, she had taken quiet a fancy to them.

These people all wore the same hats. High crowned and wide brimmed. Some had bands around the crown with exotic feathers sticking out of them.

Izabel wanted one. She wanted one immediately.

"Cuff her," the leader with the portable speaker contraption ordered his men. He was no longer using it and she wondered if it was heavy to carry around. He identified himself gruffly as Sheriff Cutler.

She was cuffed and led to a small office just off the landing field.

Sheriff Cutler leaned back in his chair, his feet up on his extremely messy desk. His boots were old and had seen some adventures, but they were still polished to a high gleam. His hands rested on the wide leather belt securing his sizable paunch.

"Speak girl. We know you ain't no Cirillean." He chuckled at his own joke. It was kind of obvious.

Izabel knew passing as a Cirillean would not be an option once she left the ship. She had concocted many lies, many fabrications, many stories.

When it came down to it, now in the moment, she simply opted for the truth.

"I am a friend of the Cirilleans. Normally," she added when he raised an eyebrow at her. "But I stole this ship from them so I could come to you. I believe the only surviving member of the first generation of my kind is here. I want to meet him. I am from Moethiica. The world of The Lady Evamiin."

"I know," he said matter-of-factly. "My Medicine Man told me all this already. And we listen carefully to our Medicine Men round here. We listen real carefully. Reg!" he shouted loudly.

Reg, the Medicine Man popped his head out from behind the screen he had been hiding very poorly behind. He too, wore one of the hats. When he fully emerged from the screen, Izabel realized just how incongruous the hat was with the rest of him. He looked like a happy, tubby, bald, oriental, monk.

Reg happily took a seat beside her. He had the most infectious smile. "Good girl you for telling the truth," he beamed at her. "He would have shot your brains out if you lied." He suddenly burst out laughing. "And your lady spend a lot of money making that brain. Shame to waste it!" He erupted into another fit of laughter.

It too was infectious. And Izabel smiled in spite of herself and the fact that it was her brain they were joking about blowing to smithereens.

"Will you let me look for him here?" she asked of them simply, as Reg un-cuffed her.

She was glad she hadn't fired those lasers on the ship, no matter what their answer might be.

Reg beamed at both her and Sheriff Cutler in turn. "Go on Boss!" he urged. "She good girl! I take her to the base of the mountain. Go on!"

"All right, all right," Sheriff Cutler said gruffly. "You can look for him. But no funny business!" He peered at her sharply.

"No funny business," Izabel agreed solemnly. "Thank you." Tears welled in her eyes. Unlike The Lady Evamiin's tears which were blue, hers were silver. "Thank you so much."

"Aw, hell. Don't you be crying now! We know you rejigged the guns and had your finger on the trigger. No good feeling all guilty now, just cause we've been so nice to you." Sheriff Cutler refused to meet her eyes now she was crying. He hated it when women cried.

Izabel was shocked. "But if you know I did that, how can you sit here so calmly! What would you have done if I'd pulled the trigger?"

"Me and Reg'd be drinking a fine ale and dancing in the afterlife!" Sheriff Cutler's eyed twinkled with merriment and he and Reg both threw back their heads and laughed.

"And next time round, you be Medicine Man and I be Sheriff!" Reg cackled.

They threw back their heads and roared, tears of laughter pouring down their cheeks.

As Sheriff Cutler recovered himself, he pursed his lips in thought and looked at Izabel. "Reg says you're one of them cytechy things." He looked a little sheepish. "You any good with computers?"

"Quite good," Izabel nodded, and her eyes were twinkling now.

"You mind taking a look at my new laptop before you head off with Reg here? Damn thing. Only got it last week. It's given me a helluva time. Hate computers."

"I will fix it for you," Izabel assured him. "And anything else you would like me to look at or fix I would be happy to. I would like to look at your codes. You have

Weeza Gremlins in your Webs. I killed one who attacked me. The body is on my ship."

"Smelly buggers!" Sheriff Cutler grunted. "That ship gonna stink. Don't you worry your pretty little head about it though. The Cirilleans take care of them for us on their big runs through."

"How long have they been invading your Webs?" Izabel asked curiously, glad the Cirilleans were on to it.

"They just come in last year," Reg said cheerfully. "But that's ok. We expect it. Big things happening at the moment. Many fighting for control. Big changes coming." He patted her hand. "You be careful on Little Blue."

"I'm not going to Little Blue!" Izabel shook her head vehemently at him, blue eyes afire. Now, more sure than ever, she would never be a part of that."

Reg just patted her hand some more and beamed at her.

"Anything you want to ask the boss for?" he asked her cheekily.

"Reg!" Sheriff Cutler drew out his name, chiding him.

"What! Go on boss, you know she going to ask anyway!"

"They don't grow on trees you know!" Sheriff Cutler barked gruffly. Which drew forth more gales of laughter from Reg.

"All right then, go on," he said gruffly to Izabel. "Ask."

Reg nodded at her frantically in delighted encouragement.

"Well," Izabel began hesitantly and then launched right into it. "I would like a hat."

"A hat!" Sheriff Cutler grumbled. "Everyone who comes here wants a bloody hat!"

Reg threw back his head and roared with laughter and his cheeks glistened with fresh tears.

Izabel sat in stunned happiness.

For the first time in her life she knew what it felt like to grin.

*****

Izabel's hat was red. She wore it proudly on the magnetic train as it sped through the countryside.

Reg sat beside her, joyously wearing his tan one.

They had sat in companionable silence for most of the trip. Both content to take in the views of the countryside out of the window.

As they slowed for a station, Reg patted her hand. "Last stop before ours. I take you to base of mountain and leave you," he chuckled. "Boss can't be trusted to run things without me." He patted her hand more vigorously. "You be fine on mountain. But you already wounded by history of your people. I think if you find this man, you be wounded more still."

She turned to him and said, "I am Cybriid. I do not wound easily."

"You are Awareness," he replied. "Your wounds as deep as rest of us."

He took her to a local shop near the station and made sure she had everything she would need. It seemed a lot to Izabel, but in all the worlds she had visited, she had never had to trek up a mountain before.

"It rainy season," Reg told her cheerfully when they reached the base of the mountain. "Maybe get a little wet."

He hugged her. Gave her final directions. "And look after hat!" And left.

Izabel travelled for many days alone, seeing no-one.

It was wet.

It was wet and hot and humid. The rains were torrential, blinding sheets of water that bordered on painful.

And when the rains stopped, the bugs came out. They bit at her ferociously, caring little that her flesh was Cybriid.

"I am real enough for the bugs." Izabel thought to herself as she doused herself in the cream Reg had insisted she take with her. It was a local concoction. It soothed the bites. And prevented scarring from the itching.

They had argued on that for a time.

"Get tattoo!" Reg had chided. "Not bug scars!"

So, she used the cream and went to sleep thinking about what image she would get for a tattoo, if she ever got one.

For the first few nights she painstakingly set up the small tent she carried. But the nights did not cool overly much and inside the tent grew increasingly rank and stifling.

In the end she settled for simply fashioning a roof over her head with the tarp. She would string it between tree branches. She got wet. She got bitten. But she was happier. She fell asleep looking at nothing but jungle and stars.

There were no systems, no Webs, no worlds, no coding. There was just her and the elements. And despite their ferocity, Izabel slept deeper than she had ever slept before.

On the thirteenth day she came across the village.

It was so green. Everything was so green. Their plateaus of crops layered like steps up the mountain.

She stayed with them for a night before continuing.

There was much jungle above them and ahead of her, they told her in pictures. Drawing images with sticks in the rich brown earth.

They admired her hat and gave her a poncho. It was made from the hair of their Llamas. Gorgeous creatures. The poncho was soft and beautiful. She rested her head on it that night and slept on it like a pillow.

For twenty-seven more days Izabel travelled up and around the mountain. The nights grew colder and she was glad of her poncho.

She found the First Gen survivor.

"I am Rafa." He said it proudly. She was the first one he had got to tell his name to in many years.

He was old and frail and at the end of his very long life.

He had aged here. His Cytech body had aged here. Like a human's. Like a real human's. He grasped her hand happily with both of his, "It has been a miracle!"

He was a hermit.

They had let him be.

He had spoken to no-one in 300 years.

His small hut and the outbuildings beside it were filled with great works of art. Paintings, sculptures, holographs.

He had spent his days lost in his art. Communing with nature and creating.

They had seven days together, before he sensed his time was ending.

Izabel sat beside him on his death bed, and knew that what she had experienced before this as feelings, were not even the shadows of feelings.

It was so intense. She choked back silver tears and tried to stay strong for him in his last hours.

"I came for the company," he explained to her as he grasped her hands tight. "I embodied in the Cybriid for the company. Bless you my child. You have been the best company I could have asked for."

Izabel howled for days.

She set fire to his magnificent creations as he had asked her to. He wanted their energy released back into the Cosmos to be born again.

He said the pleasure was in the creating and not in the gazing upon. Because the world had shifted since that moment of creation, and what had been new, was now already old.

She kept one small pendant he had crafted out of the stardust of Luciienn. The brightest star in the cosmos. The Questioner. The Light Bringer. Its huge, luminous presence in the night sky asks questions of us all.

The pendant was small and exquisite.

She fashioned it on the plain chain she wore around her neck.

When she returned to the village, she asked their Medicine Man to design a tattoo for the underside of her elbow. She wanted it to hide the opening of her needle probe.

He looked deep into her eyes and nodded. He did the tattoo himself. Tapping deep into her flesh with his ancient tools.

Izabel worked for three weeks in their crop plateaus to pay for it.

She loved it.

They had drawn its meaning in pictures in the rich earth for her.

"You are Awareness."

On the magnetic train back to Reg and Sheriff Cutler, it was a different pair of eyes that looked out of the window at the view.

She cried some more when she told them about him.

"Aw, hell," Sheriff Cutler cursed when her tears started, but they fussed over her, and saw her bathed and warm and fed. That night she snuggled, and slept sound, in a huge comfy bed.

In the morning the Cirilleans were there. Gracefully, they waved off her apologies. And assured her this world would be kept safe in what was to come, and the Weeza Gremlins taken care of.

Small and gray, with large heads and enormous eyes, the Cirilleans are as wise as they are graceful.

They listened to Izabel patiently and carefully. They agreed to her request. Yes, she could use their ship to get there. But they warned her that all were forgetting there now and none were leaving. The Webs crawled with Weeza Gremlins and worse than Weeza Gremlins. There were many players fighting for control, and many waiting eagerly for the Veil to open.

And once the Veil parted...

The Pirates could get her on. But they did not know any who could get her off.

Izabel nodded, understanding. "It does not matter," she told them. "I must be there. I must go."

In the paintings of the First Gen Survivor, the paintings of her Ancestor, there had been many themes, many visions. But in his final creations, there had been one image repeated over and over again.

And it had been an image of Izabel.

It had been an image of Izabel, in the midst of the Veil war, on Little Blue. And so, after all her protests about it, she was there anyway. But whose side she was on, was unclear.

"This is why," was all Rafa would say to her, when she asked him why she must go.

"Because my side is unclear?"

"Yes!" he smiled at her, pleased.

She had not understood it until she had to burn the final image of her on Little Blue.

It did not matter to anyone if she did not go there and did nothing.

She would just be another one who didn't do, instead of one who did.

But it might matter a lot to many, if she took a real risk, and went and did something different, to what was expected of all of them.

And this was for Izabel, as it is for all beings who ever wake up deep enough to realize the true nature of sides, the point where Awareness and she became one.

And if someone tries to make you pick anything, Awareness is always a fairly good bet, to hang your hat on.

Minx Fae

Three hours ago, world is as it should be.

Three hours ago, I recline on couch, waiting outcome of Sebastian's deal. Profit high. Almost high as dodgy. I already counting first, ignoring latter. I am Minx Fae, not burdened by lesser emotions - like guilt for gullible - so this not hard for me.

And not hard for Sebastian's gang of fools. Inept, but hot to look at. So, I's look. We in great market of Zesh. In one of gaudy pillow laden dens set aside for these things. It deliciously hot. Hookahs compete with incense. Tea spiked. Sounds of haggling, lying, cheating all around us.

Ah, market day. I am happy.

I am happy and content all things unfolding as I plan.

In words of great mother of understatement, how things change.

Because now world is most definitely not as should be.

And all because one night...is ancient history now! So long ago. But man is crazy. Still hold grudge.

Not even my fault in first place.

Was random night. On way home. Run into old friend. Go for drink. Sometimes these nights play out good. Sometimes play out bad. This start good. End very bad.

It all night hookah bar, smoke machine, nasty batch of Sprite beer. Me dancing, dancing. But I am little. I am Minx Fae. I know is not allowed but I just float up a little way. Swaying, dancing. Up a little higher. Maybe have a little twirl.

Next thing, disgusting! My left horn is with squishy!

And all hell is break loose! Crazy, angry man threatening all kinds of thing! Anger management issues indeed. And all very harsh considering is accident. And drunken accident at that. And no considering how traumatize I am in all of this!

Is disgusting having stupid, squishy eyeball on end of horn! And get off! I still shudder when think of this.

Worse, I must go in hiding when old one-eye put reward on head! I mean, I hold no grudge. I let bygones be bygones. But he want revenge. Not eye for eye. He want horn for eye. Namely, my horn, his eye.

Old one-eye not so stupid as looks. He know my horns worth fortune. Much more than stupid eye. I think is plot all along.

I am very attached to horns. They gold and white. You know how rare is with blood red wings? Is right - very! But I digress.

He no get grubby mitts on me then, and he no going to get grubby mitts on me now.

Exit, stage left.

Sebastian and gang of fools is right behind me. They is nasty firearms one-eye brings with him.

But lucks for all his aim is bad as breath. As we exit market he fire very poor shots and miss us.

Unfortunately, he take out wild Zesh fighting rock goat and intergalactic federation customs agent. There be a lot Zesh law enforcers turn blind eye to, but shooting wild Zesh fighting rock goat is not one of these things.

They worth fortune! Even more than horns. Also, they usually owned by demon lords. And nobody with lick of sense annoy wild Zesh fighting rock goat owing demon lord.

Anyways, now is men in funny uniforms everywhere. I did not even know we had so many law enforcers. And when they start giving them uniforms? How they catch us doing anything? If they make them stand out like that?

But my, these ones is efficient looking. Me begins to think not from around these parts. Still, old one-eye is giving them good chase. I think I about to see one get him, and then all hell break loose again.

As drunken demon lord career out of tavern to find favorite wild Zesh fighting rock goat dead.

Is not good to be closest bystanders when demon lord questions start. Locals know this and there is blind panic stampede to be furthest away from him and goat.

Efficient looking men appear to be not so clued up on demon lord etiquette.

They learn quick after first three deaths.

But all this lets old one-eye get away. And I is cursing fit to burst when I feel net go round me.

Efficient looking man is on end of it.

So I presume is for my protection as demon lord still on death rampage. But I no like as is playing havoc with wings. Still, I smile, not too much to show fangs - I am smarts in these things - and nods prettily at man as he perform identity scan.

And waits for hims to release me. I have paid for updated "is good" identity read only yesterday. Godds be praised!

Release does not happen.

Even after Zesh fighting rock goat proves to be sleeps rather than dead.

Old one-eye had not even shot goat! Demon lord had been in tavern for three days and goat bored. Zesh fighting rock goats capable of very deeps sleeps.

Grumpy when wakes up though. Almost grumpy as owners.

There is more death at hands of goat.

And then demon lord is happy.

Efficient looking men have learnt much. They wisely lets him and goat go on their way.

I waits for them to do same for me.

But no's.

There is no such lucks for me.

I gets put in cage!

Me! In cage!

Is disgusting. Is so small I cannot stretch wings.

Two very bad, efficient men, they questions me for hours.

Not's about Sebastian, either. No, is all about old one-eye.

Godds be cursed the night's I meets him!

And godds be cursed disgusting, squishy, fishy eyeball!

Yes, is fishy. Is very fishy. Because these men crazy for eyeball! They wants it so bad, they's bully me till I tell them where is remains.

Poor Droons. I prays he has nothings too incriminating out when's they go round there.

When they return they will tells me nothing. Only that's they gots it from him. They puts it in fronts of me - disgusting! And asks where is rest.

Rest?

If rest, is tramped into bar floor longs ago.

No's they say.

And both's of them looks thinkings at me.

Is no good. Me no likes anyone looks thinkings at me. No goods ever comes of this.

And I is right.

Is no goods they wants from me.

They get different scanner. Do more scans. Not for identity. Just on horn.

Because…

Is still in there!

Oh, hideous, disgusting, squishy, fishy eyeball! Bits of its are insides of me!

Insides my beautiful white gold horn.

I am sicks when they's tells me.

I throws up all overs them.

Minx Fae vomit. Very nasty.

A small joy. It serves them rights.

I here longs time while's clean themselves. Not so quick. Not so easy to cleans.

Hee hee.

Glee short lived.

Because when's they comes back they tells me they will opens up horn to gets out.

"Goods lucks with that," I's mutter.

Minx Fae horns very strong. Almost strong as Zesh fighting rock goat's. Or demon lord's.

"Oh, we won't need any luck," One with dark blue eyes and goods hearing says. "Not with this."

He smiles as he holds it up to me.

Is Pann blade. Can cuts through anythings. Even Pann's horns.

They backs back quickly as I's vomits again.

I's miss.

They learns quick, these mens.

"Why's?" I demands. And nows I flash my fangs. "Why's this one? Is in bits! Old one-eye stills got's other eye! Finds him! Gets that one!"

I stamps my foots. I am grumpy's now.

The blonde's one smiles at me like I am dumb fairy.

I hiss at him and breaks the links on ones of the nasty wrists chains.

They is open mouthed, staring at me.

I pulls on the nasty wrist chains harder. It breaks.

They's gasps and goes for guns.

Is vomit.

It miss them's but gets chains.

Tolds you is nasty.

Efficient's mens not so smarts.

They thinks normal wings restraints wills work on me.

Hee hee.

Very barbed and poisonous, my wings.

I's gives the nasty one with dark blues eyes a nasty tastes of them's as I flies over him.

Will hurts like bitch till morning.

The dumbs one I not hurts so bad. I is not completely merciless.

Stills, they both paralyzed for moment.

I raise alarm myself's and waits up high. Whens reinforcements comes I flies rights over them's.

They using Zesh law enforcer station closest to mains space port. I is familiar!

There is vent at end of supply corridor bigs enough to squeeze through.

I squeeze. Is not so easy as remembers it. Must stops daily eats of deeps fried scorpions. Will stops. Will just have three as treats for escaping's. Mmmm. Dipped in chocolate. Yum's.

Is all inspirations I needs. And I is through. Scraped and torn's but throughs.

Vents opens in dark, dirty corner of alley next to space port.

I smells scorpions and every instincts pulls me that ways.

Excepts one.

Damns its!

I stamps foot, but follows instinct leading away from scorpions. Is very strong's. I drawn's to it.

I keeps low as I enters space port.

Mmm. Interesting's. That is rebel ship. Incandesa3. Deeps space hauler.

I sniffs air.

There is ones on that who not show themselves to be what's are.

Minx Fae nose very goods at detecting's such things.

Minx Fae ears also very goods at hearings pursuits of efficient's mens close on trail.

I makes breaks for ship. And the godds smile on me and put scorpion eating idiot in's path.

I swipes. Is not chocolate covered, but wills do.

I heads for prison hold in bottoms of ship.

I's expects big, but's this huge. There is bigs metal ramps hangings from ceilings. Runs rights down middle. I go's up theres to have better looks.

Is mosts peculiars. They's got beds downs theres. And guards. But they's not guarding's they is lounging's.

I hear's them gets told's they beings secured's in theres and to stays quiets.

Most peculiar's. Most peculiar's indeeds.

Goods things is darks. Just greens exits lights.

I finds odds and sods and makes little cubby. Is comfy.

But I no's relax until ships takes off. Then tucks into's scorpion.

Must finds Seth. Seth will haves ways to gets eye's out of horn with no hurts. Pann Lord magics.

I is familiar of Seth, greatest of all Pann Lords.

He looks for Fifth Veil Siren now's. I's too. But I's gets distracted in Zesh. And she no there. I's sure of thats.

Hiccup.

Scorpions makes me's belch.

One of guards comes to looks. But I hides good. I is smarts likes that.

Now's guards all sleeps and I's about to joins them's.

Three hours ago, world is as should be.

Now is better.

When's world as should be is turned on ass, godds smiling's on you, no?

Hiccup.

Is all good. They no's hears me.

Is nice you worries though. I save's bit of next chocolates scorpions for you's and leaves on pillow.

Now shoosh's.

I's sleeps.

Haven

"What are you, Haven?"

There was no preamble. He simply asked the question he most wanted answered.

He was a distinguished looking man. Cultured. His salt and pepper hair was cut short in a military style. He had a military bearing.

His voice was pleasant, polite, hypnotic.

Bright eyes. They shone. And he had the ability to hold a look in those eyes that made others quickly lower their own.

It was not a particularly aggressive look. It was simply a look of I am in control here. You will not fuck with me. You will not lie to me. You will not annoy me. You will not do anything that displeases me. I will be obeyed.

And all the time they said all these things they would be shining as bright as stars in the sky. And he would be smiling. And talking. Politely, pleasantly, urbanely.

It was disconcerting and incongruous.

He was an exceptional Chief of Intelligence.

Haven looked at him through a fog of pain and aftershock.

Her head throbbed. Had they hit her? Is that what had knocked her out? She could not remember. Her wings were tightly bound, she was secured tight in a metal chair, and they had a shield grip on her. The weight of it was like mountains bearing down on you. Physically, mentally, emotionally. It made the smallest movement hard. And escape impossible. All this just for her?

She was in a small, barren, metal interrogation room.

Three Security Detail stared at her, unrelentingly, behind a clear, blast proof wall.

She could not see Soar and prayed her friend had survived. She raised her violet eyes to the urbane one and hissed at him.

He turned and gestured to the Security Detail.

The first of two doors hissed open. The automatic weapons in the roof of the room activated, simultaneously turning towards Haven. Her body immediately lit with the red hum of tracer locks.

Three Security Detail and a Security Engineer stood in the air lock between the first and second doors surveying her and the room.

Satisfied, they gave the signal for the second door to be released. It hissed back slowly, and they moved into it with a quiet, well practiced efficiency.

The Security Detail fanned out, their weapons aimed alternately at Haven's head and chest. The Security Engineer moved quickly towards her, injecting the thinnest of long needles into her arm through the shield grip. It was a paralytic with an instant effect.

She sat, frozen, unable to move, as he placed a titanium tracker on her right ankle. It's needles shot sharply into her flesh and secured themselves there. The pain of it was excruciating but she could not cry out.

The paralytic was fast acting and also fast fading. As she felt the last remnants of it fade away, the Security Engineer injected her with what felt like the queen of all opiates. This nectar was fast acting too. And so much more than opiate. Haven felt a warm rush break over her body in waves.

She felt like honey.

The Security Detail and the Security Engineer stayed in the room with her. There were more Security Detail in the room outside. There was the red hum of many weapons trained on her.

But Haven was not aware of any of this. She was in the honey world of the opiate.

She would not have moved from where she was if the doors had been wide open.

When the salt and pepper one finished consulting with the Security Engineer and sat down opposite her once more, she stared at him dreamily.

He made a small signal with his hand and the Detail in the room lowered their guns.

He smiled at her.

"My apologies my dear for drugging you to this extent," a slight pause as he appraised her. "We were unsure how much to use on a Siren."

He smiled at her again. "Now we know."

"Who is a Siren?" Haven slurred curiously.

"You are my dear. You are. Do you not remember?"

Haven frowned at him. "I am not a Siren. I am a Silff."

He smiled at her again. "Indeed. It would appear you sometimes are. We have run numerous tests. The most

advanced tests available to us. The results are...
interesting," he paused. "But when you set off the alarms
at the desert border, you set them off as a Siren, my dear,
not as a Silff." He fixed his eyes steadily on her. "Why
was that, do you think?"

"Malfunction?" Haven suggested hopefully, doing her
best to be helpful. He seemed like such a nice man now.

He nodded at her. "Well, that would be logical and
put all our minds at rest. But unfortunately, you set off
more than one. They were all testing accurately before
you. And they are all testing accurately now. And they
read your friend, Soar, as a Silff, at the same time as they
read you. So, you see why I have my concerns Haven,
and why I have to ask the question, what exactly are you
my dear?"

Haven's drugged eyes lit up at the mention of her
friend. "Soar? Is she alive? Where is she? I want to see
her." Her enthusiasm trailed off a little at the end. Putting
the string of words and questions together had been
exhausting.

"Your friend is gone, Haven," he looked at her
sharply. "She saved herself at your expense. That is
interesting, don't you think?" He laughed suddenly. "That
she should make it across the desert border to the rebels,

when, based on our tests, it is actually you they would want."

"You let her go," Haven whispered.

The man tilted his head to her in respect. "We have plenty of Silff. But so very few Sirens."

He looked at something on the screen read out in front of him and asked, almost casually, "Do you remember being a Siren, Haven?"

She frowned at him, struggling with something, with the depth of what he had asked her, as the opiate took a deeper hold in tune with the careful spaces he was leaving between words.

" How would I remember being something I don't know I am?" she asked eventually.

"Well that is the question for the ages isn't it my dear," he replied.

He rose from his chair and began to pace the room.

Haven followed his movements lazily with her eyes. Back and forth. Back and forth. Side to side. It was hypnotic.

He stopped suddenly and turned to her, "Have you remembered yet?"

"No," she said dreamily.

"What a shame," he said. And continued his pacing.

They carried on in this manner for the next hour or so.

He paced the room for several minutes at a time and then stopped and asked if she'd remembered.

And Haven dreamily said no.

At thirty-three minutes he stopped his pacing and sat back down opposite her.

The Security Detail lifted their guns to their shoulders and trained them back at her head.

The red tracer beams hurt her eyes.

The hum annoyed her.

She went to swat at it but her wrists were tied. Oh, they were tied to the chair.

She gave a little grunt of discontent.

She pouted at the hum. And squinted at the red lights.

And as she squinted her focus shifted and she was aware.

She was aware of the Forest all around her.

She breathed in deep. Savoring the rich, heady smell of the dark, chocolate earth. The emerald green canopy rose above her.

And then the world shifted and she was in indigo.

Against the back drop of an indigo sky they flew. The air was thick and heavy. Three electric blue moons shone down on them. When the dawn came, three violet suns would replace them.

But they would not see the dawn here. They would already be Off-World in the land of the Wizard. A pale, washed out world lit by a single moon and a single sun. Its Webs graying and thick. All of the rainbow colors long since gone. Leaching the land. Leaching it of its spirit and its color.

The Wizard had called them there. To fix it?

Hard to tell. Always hard to tell with a Wizard. But he had called them. And he was the Wizard of the Lighthouse. And his world home to one of the great creator spirits. And so, they would answer. They would come.

But they would not come alone. They were not that stupid.

Theiia gave the signal to Haven to prepare the others for the World-Bridge.

Haven smiled and nodded her ascent. She wheeled around to face those they had brought with them.

A thousand at least. A thousand pairs of magnificent ebony wings spanning out to the far reaches of the horizon. A thousand breathtakingly beautiful faces on bodies to make the most glorious of the goddesses weep.

Tiny horns emerging from flowing locks. Violet eyes. Glorious eyes. Eyes in which worlds were formed. Eyes in which the cosmos sang.

And what a song it sang.

Haven felt it rise in her now. Rise from the depths of her being, flooding through her heart and pouring out through her eyes.

Her vision became the vision of the cosmos. A riot of jewel colors in endless, timeless space. She saw ancient stars explode to be reborn in human form. She saw worlds form. She saw worlds die. But there was no death in this timeless dance. No endings that were endings. There could be no endings. Because there was no time.

She saw the unending, glorious, beautiful, timeless magnificence of it all. And she opened her beautiful mouth and the song sang out of her, finding voice in the bridge between worlds.

And a thousand before her took up her song and the cosmos rang with the sound of its song as only a Siren knows how to sing it.

Haven smiled and wheeled back to take her place at Theiia's side. This day it was Theiia's army. But one day it would belong to the Siren of the Fifth. The Veil Siren. Able to pierce the Veil between worlds.

Theiia smiled at Haven, knowing this also. Then she released the command to open the World-Bridge and the Sirens prepared to cross.

The world turned.

And Haven breathed in deep again.

She was back in The Forest.

Rich, heady, chocolate earth. Lush, emerald green. The air was like a drug. Just to breathe was ecstasy.

Carefully, she parted the branches with her small hand and looked out on the clearing which stood before the great ruins of Iiviithcaa.

He was there.

Leaning casually against the fountain. He threw a drez fruit in the air between his left and right hands. He did this several times before he put it to his mouth and took a substantial bite.

He chewed on it contentedly. When he'd finished he smiled in her direction, holding the fruit out to her. "Would you like some, Haven?" He always knew she was there, no matter how carefully she hid.

She edged shyly out past the bushes facing him. She always felt shy facing him.

It had taken him six months to lure her out from the bushes when she first discovered him there.

That had been some time ago now.

She crouched and launched herself in the air. Her fluffy violet baby wings were beginning to sprout adult feathers. She flew beautifully now. And when she had all her adult feathers she would fly even better.

He held out his hand to her and she placed her own small one it. Delicately he lowered her to the ground, her wings beating gently.

He sat down opposite her and gave her the drez fruit.

She bit into it hungrily, the sharp, sweet juices running down her chin. He picked up the story exactly where he had left off.

It was a strange story. It was a strange story of forgetting and power and hate. A story of fear.

But his voice was smooth and melodious. And Haven lulled contentedly on the grass beside him, calm amidst the story of hatred and fear.

He must have been telling the story for many hours when she felt a tickle on her hand and looked down to see a butterfly come to rest on her. Its beautiful wings softly beating. A rhythm to them that soothed her, brought her back to herself. It rested delicately on her small, plump child's hand.

Haven stayed very still as the panic welled in her. When had she become a child again? Who was this man? What Forest was this? Where was their army?

A song began to rise in her as if in answer.

The talking creature before her became small, ant like. Lost in the cosmic dance that played before her eyes. She could see the Webs binding him, pulling at him, fighting for control. Draining him. She knew she had the power to cut those Webs. She knew that once those Webs were cut she could sing him a song that would lead him to a golden thread.

And then the gray Webs could never touch him again.

She could sing him his freedom song.

She could sing him free.

But she was not in her normal form. And the song died before it had risen. Her vision returned to the Forest. The man before her seemed big again, and she seemed small.

The butterfly rose from her hand and brushed gently past her cheek. "Theiia!" The fleeting memory pierced her, and a sob escaped her heart.

The man stopped his story and remained silent, watching her.

"Why?" she asked him eventually.

And he smiled at her and said, "I will tell you that tomorrow."

But she had never got to hear that part of the story.

Because when she returned tomorrow everything had changed. There was no fountain. There was no story-telling man.

But there was a carving on the side of a tree.

Haven traced the outline of the carving with her small finger. And then she stepped around the tree, and happened upon a path.

She had not been down this path before. She followed it slowly and eventually came to a city. It was one of the cities from his story. And she wheeled around and launched herself in the air to fly back to the Forest. She slammed into the shield she had never known was there, and fell to the ground, stunned and landing hard. And then they were upon her.

And she forgot. She forgot everything.

Haven opened her eyes. The salt and pepper man was seated, staring intently at her.

He smiled at her. "Will you tell me more of these stories, Haven?" he asked.

"I will," she said.

And then threw up all over him.

No matter. She had given him more than he ever could have hoped for.

And she would continue to do so, now the opiate, and his own hypnosis, had their hooks in her.

Finally, they would find out exactly what these creatures were. Finally, the mysteries of the Sirens would be revealed to them.

As he was cleaning himself off in the shower, Attiicus congratulated himself once again on his interrogation method. It could get a little messy, but his theory had proven correct once again.

You catch more flies with honey.

You hear more truths in story.

And beyond the veil, in the part of the mind that consciousness forgets, the real us lies.

And if you can pierce the veil it will tell you of yourself.

And that is the best story that can ever be told, beyond all measure.

Epiphany

"A man stops his car outside of a hotel and immediately realizes he's bankrupt."

"Goddamn it!" She crumpled her beer can in frustration.

"Do you give up? Do you give up!"

"Yes, I give up! Just put me out of my misery and tell me!"

"Monopoly! It's Monopoly, you goose!"

Ear piercing guffaws from her partner.

She threw the crumpled beer can at her. Goddamn lateral thinking games. Jess delighted in torturing her with them on every goddamn stake out.

How the hell could she lateral think when that gnome in the corner kept peeping out from around the dumpster and winking at her? Wearily, she rubbed her forehead.

Note to self, Woman stops car in alleyway. Is subjected to one too many lateral thinking games by evil partner. Sees gnomes. Plots to kill evil partner.

There was definitely something in that one.

Fresh air.

She needed fresh air.

"I'm just gonna grab some air."

No response.

A snore.

A peaceful snore.

She didn't bother to look. Jess had done her miraculous schizo leap from hyper to hibernation. But hey, 10 bad beers and boredom will do that to a girl.

10:00PM.

And no sign of life from the windows three floors up. All was in blackness, just as it had been three hours earlier when they'd arrived on the job.

Apartment 3E. They'd bugged this place a month back at least. And then nothing, until now. Now, what though? It's not like they were high enough on the food chain to listen to the goodies their bugs were bringing in. And Chico wouldn't tell them anything. Just wanted them to watch and take note of any coming and goings.

From the alley!

He'd been most insistent they stay in the alley. And preferably not even move from the car.

Dullsville. So far tonight there hadn't been a helluva lot of action round the back entrance to Edgeview Heights. But hey, Chico was the boss. And if it made him feel better to keep them in the dark, and watch for comings and going from Apartment 3E from the most illogical vantage point on offer, so be it!

A girl could do a lot worse than earn the sort of cash they did from the crazy-assed assignments Chico sent their way.

She turned up the volume on the receiver to max, so that the merest murmur from CCC - Chico Command Central - would be transmitted loud and clear to sleeping beauty. Jess was cool like that. She could filter the irrelevant in her sleep. If something happened worth worrying about, she'd be hardcore awake in about three-seconds.

Epiphany got out of the car and stretched luxuriously. The black cat suit she'd chosen for this evening's shenanigans was almost sensible. Her Walter Steigers however, were at least ten blocks from the nearest sign pointing the way to the domain of the sensible.

She decided to take a little look-see down the end of the alley, which was hidden in deep shadows.

She steadfastly ignored the gnome, as she walked past him, and the dumpster.

Click clack.

Click clack.

Something crashed loudly, concealed from sight in the shadows she was fast approaching. A curse followed, dispelling any cat, rat and garbage can scenarios she might have been hoping for.

"Who's there!" She had her gun aimed and herself positioned defensively behind the dumpster, in an amazingly quick time.

"You move fast for a Walter Steiger shod, cat suited, beer drinking woman." It was the gnome. He winked at her conspiratorially.

"Shut up!" she hissed at him.

She re-focused her attention on the shadows. But there were no more crashes and curses. Silence and shadows. Not even a flinch of movement.

"Come on buddy. I got you covered here. Come on out, and let's do this the nice friendly way."

More silence.

The gnome sighed pointedly and studied his fingernails. Which were pretty gross, actually. Yellowish, long, pointed. And not all that on the clean side.

All silence. Well, apart from the gnome sighs.

"He's gone, you know." The gnome spoke slowly, with more than a little condescension in his tone.

"Oh, well, Duh!" Epiphany was not feeling in the most gracious of moods. She straightened up slowly, her gun still aimed.

The gnome pursed his lips at her in disapproval. "You're not very nice at all, are you? Quick, and stylishly attired, I'll give you. But nice? No, not so much at all."

She opened her mouth to retort, but he cut her off abruptly.

"A very rude little god-prayer indeed!"

"I am not!"

"Oh, yes you are. You're quite the rudest little thing in heels I've come across in a long time."

"Listen, short guy, I am neither little - she really wasn't, especially in comparison to the four-foot gnome - nor a "god-prayer." I think your born-again radar may be slightly out of whack there, buddy."

"Well, for someone who professes not to be a god-prayer, your everyday language use revolves rather passionately around them. You don't even pick one or call them by name!" The look he threw her was most accusatory.

"You are one weird gnome. And you don't know anything about my everyday language use. *Do you*?" Had this strange little creature been spying on her?

"I am not a gnome!" The look and hiss he threw her way were fearsome, and she recoiled in spite of herself.

He tossed his head proudly, and in a much calmer tone proclaimed, "I am not a gnome. I am an alley troll."

"An alley troll?"

"Yes, an alley troll."

"What the hell is an alley troll?"

"A being far superior to a gnome!" he snapped at her.

He looked up into the night sky as if doing some god-praying of his own, and then turned to her, "I am Klaus."

"Epiphany. Charmed I'm sure." She was finding it hard to keep the sarcasm out of her voice. But that was nothing new. Didn't really take a psychotic alley troll with delusions of grandeur to bring out that particular personality trait.

"And?" Klaus raised one expectant eyebrow at her.

"And what?" She managed to keep most of the edge out of her voice, but couldn't quite stop the involuntary tapping of one impatient foot.

"No apology, no Tour!" He glowered at her. Apparently, alley trolls could be a little short on patience too.

"What tour?"

"*The. Tour.*" The alley troll stretched out the words. And then his shoulders slumped and he looked crestfallen.

Epiphany felt bad, which in turn made her uncomfortable. Which made her want to exist the entire situation, STAT.

"Listen Klaus, I am on a very important assignment right now. I certainly don't have time for, nor do I even remotely want, any tour, of any kind, of this stinking alley. Now, as long as you, and your little shadow friend, don't give me any grief, I'll leave you to your entertainments."

She turned on her heel and made her way back towards the car.

"What do I have to do to get you people to see what's before your very eyes! Bah!"

Whoosh!

Something small whizzed neatly past her left ear.

Ok, so the alley troll was a little grumpy, but she was extremely, extremely annoyed now.

"What is your problem, troll boy! Oh!" She'd turned to face him off in the distance and nearly fallen over the little guy. He was right behind her, and he was brandishing what looked like some sort of weird-assed slingshot.

"Come with me!"

It was not an invitation.

"Listen, Klaus. A word of advice from me to you. When you're attempting to threaten a woman, armed with a gun, and trained to hurt people in lots of ways, try to have a little more than kiddy toys in your arsenal. Now, just put your little slingshot away, and I'll forget this unfortunate lapse of judgement on your behalf, ever happened."

Silence.

A tense stand-off.

"Wahh, Wahh, Wahh! Wahh, Wahh, Wahh!"

"Oh Jeez." The little psycho had fully started to cry! And for all her hard-ass attitude she was a sucker for tears.

Very awkwardly she patted his back. "Hey, come on little guy, chill. It'll be Ok. Come on, come sit down over here and tell me all about it."

Sniffle snuffle.

Click clack.

Looking extremely injured and self-pitying, and not at all like a psychotic, sling shot wielding alley troll, he allowed himself to be led to an old, overturned crate. He sniffled and snuffled some more, sighed deeply, and then launched into his tale of woe.

"I am the Bridge Keeper here. And I have been the Bridge Keeper here for 179 years. Can you imagine that! 179 years in this stinking alley!"

He was not a happy troll.

"I used to be Master of the hardest of the Crossings in my time."

"The Crossings?"

"Yes, the Crossings! Not like your petty comings and goings from A to B. The great Crossings between the worlds."

Epiphany raised one skeptical eyebrow, but he pursed his lips knowingly, and continued his tale with vehemence.

"But then suddenly, no-one was interested in the Crossings anymore. Oh, there always were, and still are, the occasional few who seek to cross, but not enough to make a living out of. And so, we were forced to the Centauri Dimension to work ordinary jobs. Industry fodder!"

He sniffled. "Which is terrible for a troll. But as the years passed, many grew happy with their new lives. But not I. I could never be satisfied like that."

He paused, and his eyes grew large and his voice awed. "And then they came for me. Came for me and told me they had a great new job for me here. That a bridge had opened between the lost city and this world. Wanted me to man it. Said once word got out, people would be streaming across it."

He fixed her with a stare and his gaze was flinty. "But do you know how many have crossed in 179 years?" He was getting really fired up again now. "Three! Can you believe it! THREE!"

"Ok, chill little guy, and let me get my head around this. You're telling me you can like fully beam me up Scotty people around the place at will?"

The troll looked at her in excitement. "No, I'm not talking about anything like a Transporter. But are you a fan? I have every series and..."

"Whoa, troll boy! Just tell me your deal in all of this." Goddamn Trekkies were everywhere. Your only hope was to be firm and head them off at the pass.

Otherwise you could be there for hours.

That had been a close one.

Klaus sighed with more disappointment and then continued.

"The bridges I work with are very specific. The bridge here is only from this alley to the lost city, and from the lost city back to here."

Two-way traffic. She could cope with that concept.

But then he continued.

"The bridges exist between worlds whose belief paradigms are at a similar development phase, and are therefore oscillating at similar energy vibrations. In the same portals."

He looked at her appraisingly.

Blinking. She was blinking very rapidly.

Abort, Fail, Retry?

Against her better judgement, she decided to go for Retry.

And start with something simple.

"Ok, so, what is this lost city? And, like, who lost it? Us? Or some other planet in the same portal thingy?"

"Worlds are not planets." There was just the slightest hint of impatience in the troll's voice. "The world of the lost city exists on many different planets as well as this one. Just as many different worlds coexist here."

"And elsewhere."

"At the same time."

He just had to add that last bit, didn't he. Epiphany shook her head, which was kinda hurting. "Ok, little guy, now you've well and truly lost me. And, I gotta say, I'm pretty happy to stay lost, at this particular point in time."

"Is Ok!" The troll was suddenly beaming and on his feet. "Better to show you!"

"Oh, no," she began. "They'll be no showing of anything..."

The look on his face stopped her flow of words.

The little guy was suddenly very still, staring at her.

The alley went dark. As in that complete inky blackness you only get in those way out in the country, night skies.

"Hey!" She spun around, trying to find a direction with at least a faint glimmer of light in it. "Hey! "Klaus!"

She sensed something approach her in the darkness. There was the scrape of brick on metal.

Clank.

Boom.

Thud.

The thud was her. Hitting the ground rather suddenly after her Walter Steigers made steady contact with a good five feet of air.

"Goddamn it!" She was going to kill that treacherous little troll.

The earth spun.

Then it somersaulted.

She closed her eyes and expected the worst.

But then all was calm.

She seemed almost to be floating in a gentle, downwards, spiral.

Whoosh!

Ok, so now it was not so gentle. In fact, not gentle at all, would be a far more apt description. She was hurtling and spiraling at phenomenal speed. She felt her stomach check out the view from her mouth more than once. Fortunately, she was highly skilled in vomit control.

And then suddenly, all was calm again.

She could hear the sound of gently lapping water.

She prayed she was nowhere in the vicinity of sewers.

"Oh!" The incredible aqua eyes, which were suddenly very close and very intense, made her jump.

"Welcome."

"Uh, hey there."

"Congratulations. You have made The Crossing. Come this way, please."

"Uh, Crossing, Ok." She took off after him, trying her best to keep up on very uneven ground in totally inappropriate shoes.

"One dead treacherous little troll," she muttered under her breath.

"Um, hey! You mind telling me where we're going?"

He smiled at her as she caught up to him and stumbled awkwardly into his arms.

He helped her into the boat. Wait, they were going on a boat now? She gripped the sides and looked around frantically, but it was like everything was misted over and unclear.

"To the island," he said. As if this explained everything.

"Oh," she said feebly.

She should have been freaking out. In a controlled, trained, focused, sort of way of course. But those eyes. They were just fire-lit.

How did she get here again?

She tried the good old trick of shaking her brain around in her head.

It didn't work of course, but the familiarity of the pointless action was comforting.

He began to row.

"We are so pleased you could take the time to come. Our belief paradigm is slipping out of the portal with your world. You will be the last to use this particular bridge crossing."

She thought suddenly of Klaus. "What'll happen to the little guy?"

"He will be well looked after," her aqua eyed host replied, smiling serenely. "He is the most gifted of his kind. If not a little temperamental," he added thoughtfully.

And then his face lit up again. "He will adore his new home. We have been trying to reach this portal for many thousands of years. There are many bridges to other magnificent and advanced worlds there."

"But not to earth?"

"No. Not to your world. Not at this time."

"Why not?" She couldn't keep a little self-righteous indignation out of her voice. I mean, Ok, we had some bad shit going down in more places than we should. We were a little bit on the rife side with greed wars, racism, bigotry and social injustice, but there was a whole other 10? Ok, maybe 9%, that was going down here.

"NAMSEs." He actually shuddered as he said it.

"Sorry, what?"

"Mmm," he nodded in affirmation. "It's definitely the NAMSEs."

"What are Namses?" She was thoroughly perplexed.

"My apologies. Acronym. New Age Movement Spiritual Elite," he replied. "NAMSE's."

"Ha! That's kind of funny," Epiphany smiled, thinking Jess was going to like that one.

"Selfies," he continued thoughtfully. "The endless pictures of first world meals - excitedly taken by the first world. Morons who talk through movies. The babies and children who may as well be on permanent social media time lapse photography there's so many photos of them splashed about all over the place."

"Oh." Epiphany didn't know what else to say. He was really on a roll now. And he hadn't even gotten to vegans or cross-fit junkies.

Although he probably figured he'd covered the vegans in the spiritual elite bit.

"You're not doing that yet, are you?" He asked her sharply.

"Uh, sorry, doing what?"

"Putting the babies and children on permanent social media time lapse photography."

"Oh! Oh, no." Epiphany screwed up her face. "Well, not that I know of." Come to think of it, she had been wondering if it was actually physically possible to take the amount of rugrat photographs some of her breeding friends did in the space of 24 hours. God, they wouldn't't, would they?

"And, then there's... well, I don't really have to say, do I?"

"What? What else is there?" she demanded.

"Hipsters," he breathed, with a level of horror normally reserved for the likes of Michael Myers from Halloween.

Or a random outbreak of plague.

And he even made a little cutting motion with his hand across his throat as he said it.

He sat back and shrugged his shoulders at her. The expression on his face said everything.

"Freaking hipsters," she muttered under her breath. "Ruining everything."

Then, she bristled.

"What about all the good things?" she blurted. "The great things? We have great things! Human triumph! Mother Teresa! Art! Literature! The Delhi Lama!"

She paused for breath, and then continued passionately.

"The Olympics! What about the goddamn Olympics!" Surely all these wondrous worlds could set aside their reservations about some dumb as a box of rocks hipsters for a bit of Olympic action!

He shrugged apologetically. "It is not my decision." He leaned forward and whispered as if afraid someone would overhear. "Those media whores with pimp-momagers and instagram addictions haven't done you any favors either." He leaned back. "Just saying."

Epiphany sighed heavily and followed his lead, by leaning back and keeping her mouth shut on the last example he'd raised. It would do no good to invoke the wrath of the pimp-momagers on these folk. One of them, in particular, was scarily omnipresent. And who knew if her dark reach extended this far?

"Ah, but here we are!" He distracted her with those fire-lit aqua eyes again and beamed as he gestured around him. "We have reached the island."

Epiphany turned to take it in.

It was breathtaking.

"Oh wow. Oh. Wow! This is awesome!"

He smiled. "Yes, we've put a lot of time and effort into the rebuilding while we've been here, and we're really pleased with the result."

He took her hands in both of his, and she almost swooned under his gaze.

"But now it is time for you to return. Take care, Epiphany Zen."

Whoosh!

Somersault.

Spin.

Thud.

The scrape of brick on metal.

Clank.

Boom.

She sat a long time in the alley. It was dark and empty and silent. Which was good. It took her awhile to get her bearings back. She was sad not to see any sign of Klaus. She would have liked to thank him.

When she opened the car door, Jess yawned and stretched her arms wide.

She was unaware of anything that had transpired. And in fact seemed to be missing the last few minutes of their most recent interaction.

"Hey, a man stops his car outside of a hotel and immediately realizes he's bankrupt." She winked at Epiphany. "Do you know what it is?"

"Yeah, it's a game."

"Oh, you know already." Jess pouted and straightened in her seat. "But do you know *what* game?" She asked triumphantly.

"Yeah," Epiphany laughed. She laughed until the tears ran down her face and Jess was staring at her like she was a crazy person.

"Jess, oh Jess, you and your goddamn lateral thinking games." She smiled as she put the car in gear. "A man stops his car outside of a hotel and immediately realizes he's bankrupt." She shook her head at the wonder of it. "Do you get it, Jess? Do you get the real answer? No, it's not Monopoly. You did it. You opened the alley portal. You made it possible."

"E, are you Ok?" Jess was looking really worried now. "Because the answer really is Monopoly."

"It certainly is. But not the board game," Epiphany replied, and then she was laughing uncontrollably again as she gunned the car away from the curb.

*****

"Well, who would have thought?" Aqua-eyes mused. "Is she trainable?"

"Anyone who can see the answer is not the board-game left as a clue is trainable," Klaus replied, and winked. "They're the real lateral thinkers, after all."

"Temperamental," Aqua-eyes muttered.

"The best of us are," Klaus huffed proudly.

"True enough." Aqua-eyes laid an arm around the lonely and ever so patient Bridge-Master's shoulders, held him close, and smiled.

Lighthouse

Dreams.

Her dreams were like honeycomb.

Like those clouds that look like tunnels of honeycomb in the skies.

And her dreams were like clouds. Floating, fleeting, fluffy and torrential.

God is in the rain. The Godds are in the rains. Which was it now? Was it one or many of them?

She could not remember.

She woke, on occasion and took in her surroundings.

She was on a beach.

She was on a beach surrounded by hills and mountains.

If she looked to the right, she could see a lighthouse.

Long deserted.

But it would flash at will.

She would be on the beach in darkness. Moon and stars the only light.

Night after night of relentless darkness.

And then the lamp in the lighthouse would begin to turn and flash.

Slowly. Unevenly. Like someone pushed it around the room.

Some of the windows were broken in the lighthouse.

And some were intact.

One time in a lightning storm, she thought she saw a face at one of the broken windows.

It was looking back down the beach.

It was looking at her.

She had stood, staring back at it.

Transfixed by shock and fear, she had not known what to do.

She had fled the beach and hidden, shivering and muttering to herself until daylight.

Every night noise made her jump and whimper.

When day came she armed herself with a stout branch. Good for clubbing. She walked one hour to the lighthouse.

She stayed in the bush and did not venture out of its cover.

She waited, silent and tense. But she heard nothing, saw nothing.

But on her way back down to the beach she felt eyes watching her.

It took every ounce of her control not to run madly away.

There were two Webs operating on this world.

The result of the botched anchoring attempts of two warring worlds new to such endeavors.

To the same, but completely different beach, the town watchman would come.

It was his town's lighthouse.

The land where the lighthouse stood, stuck far out into the sea, and up high. It had been deserted for a long time now. But still, the town was full of talk of the wizard who had been imprisoned in it all those years ago.

His ghost still pushed the giant lamp around, they said.

Not his ghost, he! Said others, who believed, because he was a wizard, he was immortal and still living.

He waits for his whores, the ones descended from those who had imprisoned him said. His whores who will bring us our destruction.

They did not like whores, and felt women should trade sex for hearth, home, co-dependence and children, instead of cold hard cash. It was how they differentiated between their women and their worthiness.

Women who did not trade sex for anything other than their own enjoyment of it, they feared most of all. Especially those who read and seemed independent. There was a town order that such creatures be shot on sight and burned on suspicion.

The same orders applied to those who preferred the company of cats.

They were distrustful of cats, perhaps sensing at some instinctive Neanderthal level that the cats were smarter than they were.

They were descended from people who imprisoned wizards in lighthouses, after all. They had not grown any additional brain cells over the generations, and were not overly bright.

And they were right about the cats, who were indeed, much smarter than they were.

The watchman rather liked cats. He fed the stray ones when he was certain no-one else was looking. Apart from that, he did not talk of it.

The watchman would come to the beach only when it was his turn.

There were several watchmen who did this. And each would often go several days before it was their turn again.

Some forgot all about it. And others would come to have a look even when it was not their go. But this particular watchman remained skittish between his turns, and did not go near the beach during this time.

The journey there would have been too much for him.

It was a magnificent beach, but it was not a beach for pleasure.

It was a beach for watching.

It was the beach where the invaders would come.

And when they came, it would be his turn. The others laughed when he said it, but he knew this to be true in the depths of his bones.

On this particular day, the sun shone, but not in an overly convincing way.

There was a bite to the air, a chill. Clouds formed themselves into whimsical shapes in the sky. And then dispersed. As if suddenly bored by their own creations.

He reached the beach and took his place, sitting down on the grassy embankment, and looked ahead.

The great creator spirit of the area opined happily in its rock creation, a mere mile or so off shore.

The sea meandered lazily in to the white sand, small waves of dancing horses breaking over the sand bars.

He looked to his left.

They were misty mountains today. Blue. Indistinct. Cloaked from view.

He looked to his right.

The lighthouse stood high and out to sea.

Wispy clouds moved steadily across the pale blue sky.

What was that! The watchmen scuttled backwards. He had seen a face at one of the lighthouse broken windows, he was sure of it.

And again!

The watchman jumped to his feet. He wrung his hands and hopped from one foot to the other. He began to shake violently.

It came suddenly into view. It had been hidden around the other side of the lighthouse.

All he could see was wings.

Huge, monstrous wings.

It was alone. It was a scout.

They had come.

He started at it for a moment. This single winged being moving slowing over the sea, towards him.

And for the first time in his adult life, in the sheer terror of the moment, he felt at peace.

On the run back to the town, feelings of elation washed over him.

By the time he fell to his knees in the town square, proclaiming his news, he was smiling fit to burst.

As the town broke into hysterics around him, he stayed in the town square grinning. He sat there for hours, his ankles crossed, his arms around his knees, his hand loosely clasped on his wrist. And he grinned.

He stayed there until nightfall.

And when they had closed and secured the city gates against all comers, he got up and paid his toll, and walked out of them.

He went to the beach.

There were thousands of them.

The wizard's whores had come.

He walked to the lighthouse cliff.

He walked right up to the edge of the cliff and kept walking.

He wanted to feel the sweet rush of air, and the warm beating wings and hot flesh catch him and enfold him.

Everybody thought him a fool.

*****

Violet eyes. They were violet eyes. Violet eyes flecked golden.

They had closed in pain. And now they opened in fresh waves.

They closed again. Perhaps opening them had not been such a good idea.

The one who had…she cried out in spite of herself…at the memory and pain of what he had done to her.

He turned to her, but he was already distracted.

His real violet eyed trophy was in play, the Third Gen had rebelled, the Siren Army had amassed into action behind the Veil.

And the Fool of the Major Arcana had jumped.

She smiled as he moved towards her again. There was no pain that could surpass bearing witness to this.

When her blood started to flow again under his attentions, she barely felt it.

She had not been who she had thought she was.

Had not lived out the life or the fate she thought she was meant to live.

She would die here tonight. In agony and humiliation.

But she had born witness to the first baby steps of a Cosmos remaking itself in an image worthy of its magnificence.

And she had pierced the veil of her own mind and seen herself. Heard her real story.

She was not a Siren. She was not a Rebel Leader. She was not the Veil Siren. She was just a girl with wings who had lived a hard life, had done the best she could, for who there was no great glory or fame or future to unfold.

A great weight lifted from her.

And when she exhaled and jumped, the great beating wings and warm flesh caught her and enfolded her. And they sang her a song of her own magnificence. And she was at peace because she to herself was finally worthy of that peace.

And the Veil parted and an even truer story was told.

Earth

Ari finished reading the report and nodded to his Senior Analyst who vanished it with a quick swipe of his hand on the central console.

For god's sake, get a grip, Ari thought to himself as Dhruv brought up a new image.

"He's a loose cannon. A high-risk connection they hoped never to have to use," Dhruv paused for emphasis. "But he is still one of them. And they are running out of options. They have put him in play."

Ari nodded again, letting out a long breath. The Senior Analyst did not need to say more. And last month, even last week, this news would have both horrified, and excited, him.

What the world did not need now was loose cannons. But the fact that they knew who this particular loose cannon was, and what was planned for him, meant they had a very real chance of stopping this new madness - that was the exciting bit - before anything too horrific went down.

That is, if the almost sabotage level of management in here didn't screw things up again. Whose side were they actually on? He wondered again. It was a constant thought these last six months. Where were they finding these people? Why were they bringing them in here? Why were they letting them *screw* things?

Ari rubbed his forehead and the sides of his face with his hands. The last six months had been bad. Cluster fuck bad. But in the last three days, the world had tipped on its head for him. Everything seemed distant. Superficial. And he was hearing things. Things that didn't make sense. But they were important. More important than the image on the huge wall projection in front of him. More important than the sabotage management screws ups. Way more.

He wished he had someone to talk to. Hell, he wished he had a bunch of people to talk to.

But there were few here experiencing connection to the Makers. Few feeling the rolling waves of anchored awareness. None of this new age or yoga-nazi shit. Actual awareness. Actual connection to the Makers. Stuff that would send way too many of the new agers and the yoga-nazis screaming for the hills.

That thought made him smile.

But the lack of people to talk to about this shit did not.

He got why bad news sells now. He got why dumb fucks got off on their petty little gossip. If you can't feel the thrill of the real and the good, you'll just settle for the thrill of the bad. Because everyone was hunting the connection. Everyone was hunting the thrill. Everyone was more than capable of anchoring to it.

Unless they gave their anchor point away. Sold it not even to the highest bidder, but the easiest one. The ones who would do all their thinking for them, define their choices for them, spoon feed their shitty little, carbon copy, lives to them.

"You will advise them there are Elementals with current high activity readings in their immediate vicinity. Which there are, incidentally, so be careful."

"Sorry, what was that last bit?" Ari's voice was hoarse, the shake barely perceptible.

But this Analyst had worked with Ari a lot over the years, and he was sensitive to changes in him. "We've established a two-man 24/7 surveillance Op, here," Dhruv indicated a place on the map now displayed on the wall in front of them.

Ari nodded from underneath his hands, and tried to breathe, very, very deeply and very, very calmly. His Senior Analyst had not just said anything about freaking Elementals with high activity readings. But to Ari it sounded like he had.

"Are you Ok, Sir?" Dhruv looked at him in concern. Ari had not even looked up at the screen.

"Yeah. No. Sorry." Ari rose. "I need to get some air. I'm gonna get Jenkins to take point on this one. I uh, I might need to be away for a couple of days."

"Ok Sir, no problem. I can bring Jenkins up to speed."

"Thanks, Dhruv. Great work by the way. I appreciate it."

Ari hurried from the room, blasting out a formal notification on his phone on the way to Jenkins' desk.

"Jenkins, you're taking point on the Boker-Shield case. I need to be out of here for a few days. Dhruv's waiting for you in briefing room one."

Jenkins raised an eyebrow at him, "Sure. You Ok?"

"Yeah. Just need to sort out some stuff. Call me if you need anything. I'll see you in a couple."

Jenkins smiled, "I'll try not to. Red alert, incoming. Cluster fuck bitch from hell approaching at high speed to the rear." He said it without breaking conversational rhythm, or giving any indication that he could see her coming.

Of course, they were trained in this. Pity now, they were using it on their own.

It was a satellite office. Sometimes the people in charge of these little satellite operations are legends. Sometimes they are morons.

Unfortunately, cluster fuck bitch from hell was high in the moron category.

And moron is Ok if morons are content to leave the efficient people with brains around them alone to get the job done. But when they get all antsy and bitter and paranoid about the efficient people with brains, and start falsely allotting credit for their achievements to their dumb sycophants, well then the good people tend to leave. And take their brains and crazy-assed efficiency with them.

Cluster fuck bitch from hell had a foul energy, a heavy, draining presence, and beady, resentful, eyes. The bitterness monster inside of her was steadily sated by the continuous cocktail of wine and prescription medication she fed herself.

Ari wondered idly what her pill to wine ratio was on a nightly basis, and hoped she maintained it. She was scary enough when she was off the happy meds, and her eyes had that permanent prescription torpor. So wrong. He was crazy sensitive to it of late. It was like looking into the eyes of something from the exorcist.

He raised his eyebrows at Jenkins.

"I'll see you," he said and made a quick break for it.

He made good speed and closed the front door on the horrific sound of his name on her lips. It was not something he heard often. He was one of the efficient ones with a brain that made her bitter and insecure, so she tried never to mention his name or much acknowledge that he even worked there.

God, she really was a disgusting piece of shit, Ari thought, as he waited impatiently for the lift. "Wouldn't piss on if she was on fire," was how he, Jenkins and numerous staff, both long gone, and present, liked to put it.

He heard the click clack of her ridiculous heels and felt the oppressive bitch from hell miasma roll inexorably towards him. She'd made good time for someone in stupid shoes. Lucky said shoes and any hard floor surface tended to give her approach away, repeatedly. It's kinda like those bells they put on cats, Dhruv had mused once, and he smiled, remembering it.

He resisted the instinct to wait to give her the finger and opted for the stairs. No need. Life - and every sane staff member currently to the rear of her - was already giving her the finger in abundance.

He pushed open the heavy door. It was one of those strange ones from Blue Earth. With funny, handles and gaps that let cold air and noise in and out in equal measure. And it had a funny opening into the stairwell action rather than sliding neatly into the wall.

WTF?

'Blue' Earth?

Where the fuck had those thoughts come from?!

Ari took the stairs at a run. Maybe it was just this place. These people. Maybe he just needed to get the fuck out of dodge for a little while and everything would be Ok again.

Maybe he shouldn't fucking drive?

Nah.

He'd just get behind the wheel and turn the radio up, and keep the window down, and drive like a motherfucker until he made it home.

Then he was going to crack open a beer and listen to some rare blues.

Then he was going to wake up whenever he damn well felt like it.

Then he was going to get back in the car and drive up to the old lake house and go fishing for the weekend.

Now, that, that was a plan.

That was a good plan.

The best laid of 'em, of mice and men, is what they say isn't it?

As Ari sat on the plane, one way ticketed to the destination that had been calling his name loud and clear for months now, he wondered when he'd get to see the lake house again.

A woman across the aisle, practically identical to cluster fuck, was pursing her lips into classic cat bum, and giving the flight attendant hell.

Ari smiled. He was sure never coming back here to go back to that office.

*****

Paige didn't remember much from that time.

The odd, happy day at the beach. The occasional camping trip.

What she remembered most was being trapped in her head. Of being unreasonably upset about things she couldn't change. And of being numb and unmotivated about things she could.

Change, that is.

Mostly she remembered how most of the time it seemed very important to play her assigned part in the life that had unfolded, almost unwittingly, around her.

Yes, there was safe. Safe was good. It was just a shame that the safe made her feel so numb.

So, when she felt the new vibrations, she knew that her safe had had a bit of a jolt. And that her numb safe was neither quite so numb or safe anymore.

She didn't know how.

She didn't know why.

But it put her in mind of the dragon shop.

In country Qld, Australia, there is a section of road between the coastal towns of Boyne Island and Agnes Waters that contains - or used to contain - a property with a sign proclaiming there are dragon eggs on the premises.

The section of road is actually a section of highway difficult to slow down on, let alone stop.

And it's a section of highway that generally means you're at a stage in your trip where you don't want to stop. The lure of the car has taken over. You want to get where you're going or get home.

These two things make it an unlikely place to ever have large numbers of cars pulling off the highway - it does seem like a rather fraught with danger and potential car crash type of place to do it - to check out said dragon eggs.

But the main reason people don't stop - apart from the indeed warranted and quite sensible car collision apprehension - is that they don't believe it.

Oh, they believe it in a sense. They just don't believe that what the sign is proclaiming is that there are actual dragon eggs there.

Even though the sign does come with a cute picture of a dragon on it, so you never know.

But they think, rather, that it will be some quaint little craft shop with hand painted eggs. Or some cute name for a manicured pot plant, or a boiled egg with chili or the like.

And while someone may be willing to risk a potential car collision, or endure the inconvenience of an unplanned detour to see a real dragon and a real dragon egg, they were not going to do it if they believed there were no real dragons, or their eggs, on said property.

Of course, there was many a car passenger, well perhaps only a handful come to think of it, who fervently hoped that there were real dragon eggs on the property. And this hope made them want to stop.

They were prepared to be disappointed in what they found.

But they were also prepared to be ecstatic in what they found. They were prepared to find dragons. And they were prepared to find dragon eggs.

Invariably these people were imprisoned in cars with those who held no such hope, and who's only belief was that there were no dragons, or their eggs, and they must press on! Get home to watch the telly or have a little nap. Fall asleep.

But what if there were dragons there?

What if there were little baby dragons poking their heads out of big purple dragon eggs?

What if there was a big mother dragon nearby? And if you were one of the lucky ones, would they take you to see her?

When Paige was little, her family used to take her to a small country town in South Australia, that had a Bunyip cave by the river. If you put 20 cents in a machine, the bunyip would rise out of the ground in the cave and scare the bee Jesus out of you. As a child, the Bunyip looked very big and very real.

It was quite possibly the best thing that many children had ever seen. Paige didn't remember much of what she spent 20 cents on as a child. But that bunyip was one of them.

They were chased off the last time they were there. Told it was offensive to the indigenous people of that area. Paige was genuinely sorry if it was, and felt awful. She'd meant no harm and no offense. She just thought the Bunyip was wonderful.

This same town also had a fish and chip shop that sold $2 worth of chips that would feed a family of five, and were quite simply the best chips in the world. Paige could still taste those chips thirty years on. They were still the yardstick she used to measure all chips, and she was yet to find their equal.

There may have been many towns with chips as good, if not better. But at the end of the day, if you don't stop, get out of the car and have a look around, you won't know.

You won't know that a Bunyip which rises from a cave for 20 cents is awesome but offensive. You won't have met those people who told you that, and chased you away from the Bunyip, and offered you a different interpretation of the world.

You won't carry the taste of the best fish & chip shop chips in the world with you for thirty years or more, and hope to meet their equal for $2 to feed a family of five.

And you won't ever know for sure that there weren't real dragon eggs on that nondescript property on that awkward piece of Qld road.

Of course, even if you do stop and check it out, you still might not know for sure.

Because if you're with one of those non-believery types who didn't want to stop in the first place, and just wants to get home and do something practical like watch the telly, then Paige believed they might hide them.

As a precautionary measure. All part of the vicious circle of only seeing what we believe and then only believing what we see.

If your beliefs are off, or a bit limited or dumb, you're screwed!

But on the bright side, you're likely to plod through life not seeing anything too challenging.

Paige had not thought about these things for a long time.

But now with the new vibrations, Paige felt a powerful calling to uproot, pack a suitcase and leave everything behind. She had a sense that she needed to be across the other side of the world. That something was coming she should be close to. Be a part of.

Which would have been nice for a change. Because often Paige didn't feel a part of things at all.

But this surge of purpose only lasted a few days. And then the longing for the safety and the numbness returned. And long used to winning over all else, they simply took up their victor's mantle with ease again.

Paige settled back into her comfortable old routines.

The first night the Elemental came, she stood at the lounge room window and drew back the curtain. Peering out into the dark night and wondering what was out there.

And then seeing nothing, she began to worry some hobo or freak was outside, watching her looking out. And she pulled the curtains tightly closed, and checked all the locks on the doors.

Unseen, and now curtained off, the Elemental pulled back from the glass. Thoughtfully.

There was bush over the other side of the road across from the house.

It liked bush. It would wait there.

Because that's the thing, and the Elemental knew this. Sometimes life lets you plod along in safe and numb until the end of days.

And sometimes it picks you up kicking and screaming from safe and numb and plops you down, often quite unceremoniously, somewhere different.

Paige was about to get plopped.

And the Elemental could wait.

<u>Scream</u>

There was a crack in the window pane. It distorted the view of the yard outside, down below. Not that there was much to see.

Hard packed red dirt. A broken swing set. A couple of rough, splintery, wooden benches.

Unbearable even to sit on fully clothed.

Excruciating with your clothes ripped from you, your body exposed. Rubbed raw and bleeding against the wood. The splinters embedding themselves in your naked flesh as you struggled to escape.

Pain.

It hurts. Passes. Scars. Heals.

Everything heals.

If you allow it the grace to do so.

Sola had repeated it often to her, smoothing back her hair and shushing her cries. It was Forest wisdom. Even Vanquish could remember it. It was the only thing of the Forest she could remember.

Grace.

Allow Everything the Grace to be done by Grace.

Sola said it to her here. But who had said it to her in the Forest? She did not know. That bit she could not remember.

Not that it mattered anymore. Four times she had escaped and tried to penetrate the shield back in to the Forest. Four times shot down, brought back and punished more brutally than the last.

And nothing.

Her Forest family did not come for her. No-one came for her. No-one came for any of them.

But each time she had seen the violet eyes staring back at her. They knew they existed here. Did they know what was being done to them?

Of course, they did. She could not delude herself on that count anymore.

Did they think the line which could not be crossed with them, was enough? Did they think the curse that came into play if they were overly dealt with while they were still children, was sufficient? Did they think that was compensation for what the Echelon did do to them when they came of age?

But the Echelon did not take all of them, did they? Only the females. And only certain females. With something in them only the Echelon could discern.

Perhaps, the Forest Silff thought this fair trade. To sacrifice these so that the rest may live and not suffer.

Live! Vanquish scoffed. With wings bound and almost every freedom curtailed. In the ghettos where they were tolerated and afforded the most meagre means to survive.

The only way out was to fight. In the underground world of the Fighters Guild, for cash and fortune.

Or with the Rebel Alliance, for freedom and glory.

Not a few, tested their skill in the first. The winged are natural fighters. Even with wings bound, they are not to be taken lightly. But with wings unbound, what a spectacle their battles make.

It is a path that proves very tempting. But even when she was young, she was certain, that for her, it would be the Rebels in the desert.

But here she was. Not in the desert with the Rebels, but still here in F-Sector, her only mission to school and guard these free-childs. Those not come of age, that could not be harmed. And as far as possible ensure that what was done to her, did not befall another.

Vanquish shivered, watching the swing move jaggedly in the wind. The remnants of a sand storm sweeping the desert.

The swing had creaked that night, cloaked in darkness. A pitch so black she could not see who stood before it.

But they could see her.

She reddened at the thought and pushed it away from her. That is how she coped with that night. Pushing it far from her, whenever the bits of it that were still too much to deal with, came too close.

*****

She had come of age shortly after midnight on that night three years ago. She was not aware of this. None at F-Sector were. A clerical error during a system malfunction. They had made a manual entry on her birth record and gotten it wrong. Twenty-One instead of Twelve.

She had another nine days, she thought, and she had her plans to escape to the desert, already in place.

Could she have done it earlier she would have. But one does not make the attempt at the desert border crossing in isolation. There are beings to be paid off that one does not short change and live to tell about it.

It would take her another three days of the disgusting, horrid jobs she performed here and there, to finally have enough to pay what was required of her.

Four of them.

They dragged her from her bed as soon as her real age turned.

Identical, black visored horrors. The helmets hid every trace of their humanity. The black needle probes which fed into their pineals connected them to each other, and to those who controlled them. They put them on and became something else.

Vanquish screamed for Sola and Theft. She kicked at the Echelon and did nougat but send the meagre belongings on her nightstand flying.

No-one helped her. No-one came for her.

Down the stairs and through the doorway to the yard they carried her as she screamed. The still, sweet, cloying air of night hit her. There was no moon. And the yard was in darkness.

But as they dragged her closer to the benches and swings, some of the black shadows parted, and she realized there were more of them, cloaked and visored.

She saw the smoldering remnants of a pit fire. Thick candles dripped black wax on red earth. Vanquish turned in the direction of soft mewling and gasped. They had a firebird, rare, sacred and beautiful. This one was bloodied and distressed, its eyes wild and its pulse beating erratically.

It looked pleadingly at Vanquish, and her heart broke that she could not aid it. She could see now they had chained it cruelly, its wings bent back at sharp angles.

She struggled furiously.

But they had the gag ready. It was laced with something. She could smell it keenly under her nose and feel it tingle against her lips. Whatever it was, it was potent.

The firebird whimpered.

The clouds broke then, and the full moon washed over the yard and made her pray for darkness. There was so many of them. And there were other things.

Mercifully, her prayer for darkness was answered. They shoved her forward towards the fire and she felt its light and heat wash over her. One of them threw a powder on it and the flames flared blue and violet. The smell was sweet and sharp all at once and her eyes began to water.

Her wrists were bound tight behind her. The rope cut into her flesh, and the grip two of them still kept on her upper arms was bruising. But it was all that kept her upright. The drug on the gag took her legs out from under her.

He was cloaked and visored identically to the others, but the way they parted for him, she knew he must be some form of leader.

He stopped very close and tilted his head at her, studying her.

He was so close to her she could feel the heat from his body dance between them.

His black, gloved hand shot out and took her hard about the throat.

Vanquish fought to draw breath and thought she was done for.

But he was merely holding her while they secured the blindfold.

He lessened the strength of his grip around her throat when they had it in place, but he did not remove his hand.

As she took painful breaths, she felt the night air on her bare skin, and knew suddenly, awfully, that they had disrobed her.

Something cold and metal was placed against her. It was long. The top of it rested between her breasts, the base of it pressed into the top of her sex.

The cold metal pulsed with magic and Vanquish felt like all the forces of the cosmos were teasing her, flicking at her, preparing to enter.

And something inside of her rushed to meet it.

The forces met. And exploded.

There was a moment of pleasure so intense it was unimaginable. And then it became too much and Vanquish felt like she would literally burst apart from within at the force of it.

He pulled away from her then, taking the cold, metal with him.

Vanquish gasped as it left her. The feeling of it parting from her was unbearable. The force inside of her which had exploded against it leapt out at it.

The voice was faint at first. In her head it spoke to her. Filled her mind with its presence. It sounded almost amused at her situation. And underneath it was a song. She knew this song. She had heard it in her dreams before.

"Easy, child. Back to yourself. Easy, now," the voice calmed her. She became more aware of her surroundings. She could hear them talking now.

"There is something about this one."

"Yes, but she is not the one."

"A pity. A great, great pity."

"Yes, but the night need not be wasted. She is not the one, but she has magic a plenty for us."

"And she is exquisite."

"Bring her here. Let me taste her."

Vanquish's calm vanished. And the voice was silent.

The ones behind her pushed her roughly. And others were there to catch her roughly and pull her down hard on to a bench.

They worked her bare back along its jagged surface.

Her tightly bound wings cushioned some of her skin. But the parts that didn't, ripped against the wood, sharp splinters embedding themselves deep in her flesh.

And her wings. She could feel the edges and feathers tear.

Fear over-rode all else. Godds, what did they want from her!

And in that moment of despair and unknowing, they had the opening they wanted.

She heard the swing creak as he pushed past it. And as he came at her in a rush she felt the mind splinter.

And it put the physical splinters of the wooden bench to shame.

The tingle of connection at the base of her skull lasted only a second. Then she felt him push his way into her, ripping through the defenses of her mind like they were nothing.

The pressure on her brain was enormous. He was ruthless and brutal.

They had the cold metal on her again now. But this time they did different things with it. Things which brought shame greater than pain. And terror which made her earlier fear pale in comparison.

As she felt her mind begin to break.

She realized this was what they wanted.

And she realized, even in the midst of this, she still had a choice. Still had options. Because there was a tiny part of her that could never break, no matter what was done to the rest of her. The voice held this tiny part of her up for her to take it. Not for long. A mere mili-second.

In most, it would go unnoticed. But most were not aware this tiny part of themselves even existed.

Vanquish had not been aware, prior to this briefest mili-second of time. But the Echelon were correct, there was something about her.

And in her awareness and the voice's offering she grabbed at it. Took that tiny part of herself and anchored herself to it.

The Echelon currently working her, felt it and grabbed at it also. But he was too late. And she heard him growl in frustration.

"What?"

It was the other who had held her by the throat before.

She felt, rather than saw, his presence stride towards her.

Roughly, he pushed the other Echelon away from her as he ripped the blindfold from her. He held her chin tight, staring deep into her eyes.

Eventually he grunted and released her. "You fools," he said quietly. "Finish it." He added over his shoulder as he strode away from her again.

And she felt a part of her essence taken then. As much as they could take. But it was without that one bit they truly desired.

But still, it was enough.

And she knew that the little they did have they would use for their magic.

And she knew also, that she would never fly again and that her wings would be useless.

Sorrow engulfed her.

Distantly she heard the firebird cry and its hot blood hiss on the flames when they sacrificed it.

Then one of them was above her with a clenched, gloved fist that came down hard and true, and she lost all consciousness.

She awoke in the med bay, lying on her stomach.

Daylight through the windows. The nurse finished whatever she was doing to her back, and left her, saying nothing.

It hit her in the stomach, almost physical, the memories, the terror and the darkness.

It threatened to engulf her but the voice was there again. "Easy. Back to yourself, child. Easy."

And underneath the voice was the song.

The darkness lifted. Not completely, But long enough for Vanquish to open a box for it. She would hide it in there. Keep it tucked away safe and sound. Away from her. Away from everyone.

They did not come back for her.

It made no difference. Still, she did not sleep.

At first, because she was terrified. The terror would never leave her completely. But over time, much time, the sharp thrusts of it dulled to a throb. She slept light then and would wake at anything. Any small noise on the stairs. The slightest creaking of the swings down below.

But Vanquish was Ok with this. Because this was her mission now. She would not leave F-Sector. She would not take herself to the ghettos to live and die pointlessly among Moethiica's forgotten.

No, she would stay here and help the others. The other Silff children they dumped here. She would teach and she would guide and she would sleep lightly.

And if anyone kicked their meagre belongings off their nightstand and screamed her name, she would be there for them.

She would answer their screams. She would join their plight and fight for them. She would not be able to stop the Echelon, that she knew. But anyone who screams deserves to be answered, to be fought for. To know that at least one other will stand with them against the terror and say, "You are not alone here."

It was not the Rebel Alliance in the desert.

But it would do.

Sprite

Even in the daylight she could see them.

Yet another advantage to living deep in the Forest. The night sky and all the wonders it revealed remained visible in the day time hours. Muted, but visible, still.

And so, she saw it rise again after all these years.

Blue Star.

An age had passed since she last beheld it.

An age since the inverse portal pulsed in the ground beneath her feet.

An age since the last Veil Siren. That had been the Fourth.

This one, now, was the Fifth.

All thought the first four had failed. But they had not. They had succeeded. They had done exactly what they were supposed to do in paving the way for this one.

This one, this Fifth Veil Siren, she had it all to do before her. No matter what had been prepared for her, her task was great. And difficult. And there were no guarantees. Ever. For any of them.

But if she failed had she not succeeded on a different level? Did it not simply mean that a different master plan was now in play? When all beings exist in a realm of endless possibilities, can there ever be failure? Can it even exist?

The inverse portal buzzed angrily underneath her and Moethiica loped sideways and spun a little faster, on its axis, in response.

Outside of the Forest, the more aware would have had felt an odd sensation, and perhaps a moment of giddiness.

Here, within the Forest however, the world spun and loped like a wild hurdy-gurdy ride.

She laughed delightedly and stamped her feet on the ground.

The inverse portal had a successful outcome in mind for itself, that was for certain.

It was getting louder by the day. It hummed on the gentle Forest breeze, so loud the last few nights it had kept her awake.

It was almost so loud now she had to strain to hear the whisperings of the tree she rested back against.

The tree was telling her of Forgetting Worlds. Not the innocent Forgetting Worlds which were a treasure and a prize. But the captured Forgetting Worlds. Like Blue Earth and Red Marza. Where the Forgetting was manipulated to serve other causes.

Where her sister would soon be landing.

Deep in the heart of the enemy.

In a world where most see and hear and touch and feel only what is expected of them. What is programmed into them. And what is programmed into them is usually the most absurd of illusions.

They fight for them.

They fight for the illusions. They fight to keep themselves enslaved.

Be-spelled, enslaved and miserable enough to fuel industries which sell them what can never be bought.

That is quite a thing to forget. That what you seek cannot be purchased.

Some accuse it has been taken from them.

She stamped her feet some more and howled with laughter.

The inverse portal did not whirl again, merely grunted.

Because it knew, as well as she, that it was never taken. It was given up willingly. They may deny it, but there is that small part of them, which is also the largest part of them, which knows.

And so, in the end, when it is taken from them permanently, there is no-one to blame but themselves.

For that is the game now on Blue Earth. That is what the big guns are playing for. To take that part permanently and never give it back. To harness it and use it to open the path to the Other Cosmos. And then Blue Earth will simply be the gateway to war. Not a war of worlds. But a war of Cosmos.

The Forest Sprite had lived a long time and seen many things, many wars. But she had never seen a war between two Cosmos.

And still the tree whispered to her of her sister.

And the part she would play on Little Blue.

It was a more complicated part with harder choices, than she perceived her sister currently imagined.

Than any of them imagined.

And then there was the other. And what a part he would play. Would she recognize him? Would he recognize her?

She was unsure.

And the tree seemed undecided also.

Is this what they hoped to achieve, though?

Did they even know what they hoped to achieve?

Had they ever put stock in such things, as the knowing of them?

On that the tree was decidedly undecided.

And she was also.

The Sprite who pondered such things had long, pale blonde hair down to her waist, secured off her face behind high, pointed pixie ears which held many piercings. Her skin was a deep golden, and her eyes, violet. She had dainty, cat like fangs, and tiny black horns.

Aside from her face, you would be hard pressed to find an inch of her not covered with the markings of her tribe.

She wore these very proudly, as all the inked Sprites do.

She was seated on the floor of the Forest, her back resting against one of the goddess trees. All the trees talked, but the goddess trees were her favorites. She liked their constant chatter when they were talkative, and their complete and utter silence when they were still.

Most of all she liked the riddles they gave for answers.

It would be highly disappointing to ask questions such as she asked, and ponder things such as she pondered, and have someone matter-of-factly answer, "Oh, that? It's just this." Or some other such boring thing.

The trees amplified the comings and goings of the Cosmos.

She might have missed the Cybriid's naughtiness completely if she had not been sitting amongst them in the grove.

She had come here to see where her sister was at, in the heart of the enemy. Catching the Cybriid in action had been an added bonus.

For the Cybriid had her part to play also. And that was already well in motion. She wondered if they would ever meet? Her sister and the droid.

The riddle the tree whispered in response was incomprehensible.

She got to her feet, brushed herself off and patted the goddess tree affectionately.

It had been a highly productive morning. She had much to report. There were many elements to a Pann Lord pattern strand. Several of those elements were now in play.

The powers that would be would be most interested.

The Sprite paused. To which of the powers that would be, would this be the most interesting she wondered. To which of these powers that would be, should she honor with such intel?

The goddess tree mumbled something about honoring none of them.

The Sprite looked to the East and concurred.

It would seem that at least one of these powers that would be, had taken it upon itself to try to kill her, after all.

Sighing heavily, she dropped to the ground and began to fashion a sling. Not an everyday, average sling, but a sling worthy of a Sprite who talks to goddess trees in an inverse portal glen.

She could hear the hum of the approaching drones. Humans thought them silent. But she had pixie ears, which as it turned out, were very handy things for hearing drones.

Ah, ready.

The first shot from the drones slammed into the goddess tree mere inches from her.

The goddess tree grunted indignantly, and the inverse portal whirled so fast and at such an angle, that even the Sprite toppled a little.

Which was fortunate.

Because if she hadn't, the second shot from the drones may well have got her.

Outraged, she stamped her foot and shook her fist at them.

That made her smile. She had always wanted to do the fist shaking thing, but had been warned that most took it badly.

But drones, on the other hand.

Poor drones, the thought took her unbidden, as the third shot took just the tiniest bit off the tip of her left ear.

Ow.

Sighing heavily, she refocused her attention on the task at hand, made a slight reconfiguration to her intention, and released the sling.

Perfectly.

Dazed and confused, the drones wondered what they had been doing here. If drones could shrug, they would have shrugged, said, "Whatevs," and gone to get a beer.

Being drones they simply meandered their way to the nearest charging station. Well, actually it was probably the furthest charging station. By the time they got there it was nightfall. They plugged themselves in and spent a merry twelve hours getting juiced up on expired drone charge, created for the much bigger model which had preceded them.

By the time they were tracked - and this was several weeks later - they were ruined as functioning drones.

But happy as fark.

They went on to spend a happy couple of years on a local recycling heap, reminiscing between themselves, and telling all and sundry about the magical jungle juice that had changed their drone lives forever.

When the time came when they both knew death was imminent, they prayed that it would come simultaneously for them, and they would not be left, one without the other.

And when it did come, it did its level best to do so. Still, the drone who had fired the first shot, felt that momentary pang of loss and extreme loneliness, when his companion was taken before him.

But in those horrid, grief stricken seconds, he was also filled with the vision of a space Sprite. She was an exquisite creature, even with a bit missing from the top of her left ear. And when she became aware of his presence, she stopped her conversation with a goddess tree to wink at him.

And then there was nothingness.

And then there was peace.

And then there was home.

<u>Night</u>

Night, beautiful night, I adore you. The quiet becomes mine. This time becomes mine. Eddies and whispers in the night. The waves of creativity flowing. The whispers of the muse finally heard. In the quiet. In the silence. Waves breaking on shore. Waves breaking all around me. Body has moved. Night movement. Night rising. Creation channeled, sourced, embraced, received, heard. The night speaks. It speaks of beauty. It speaks of adventure. It speaks of surrender. Veils part. And those that would hide in its cover show their beautiful eyes. Winged creatures with button faces and bright eyes wing a beautiful grace dance through its skies. Night grace. Night wings. Night dance. Night eyes. Winging. Beating. A gray, membranous glide. Furry. Button nose. Wings stretched like leather. Night eyes. Such beauty. Such wonder. Such magic in your shadows. All things are possible. All things are possible. All things are possible. The different self which will open in the dream landscape starts to rise. The landscape of your dreams. What beauties, surprises and riches does it hold tonight? The veils begin to part. The dreamscape begins to form, to prepare itself. For this other you which pulls riddles apart like bones and snap! It finds another riddle. Just for you.

<u>Origin</u>

When the first Federation ship landed on Blue Earth it was the time of the first incarnation of the Saurs.

Back then, there was no real day and no real night.

Only a relentless indigo.

Indigo and madness.

And in the madness, there were great beings who gathered around fires that burned without cease. Fearless, foolhardy beings, filled with power and portent and magic.

They had come for the Godd Mists. They were the strongest set of Godd Mists detected in an age. And when ones like these blow through a world, no matter how far from the rest of the Cosmos that little world may be, those who live for such things, come from everywhere.

They come to ride them.

Or they come to bare witness.

The great beings around the fires had come to ride them.

Dasha had come to bare witness.

She had begged to come here. The first anthropological mission to this planet, at a time like this, no less! Who, in the Cosmos would be drawn by these Godd Mists? Who had the capability now, to get here and transition successfully on this world?

They had given her only the smallest of teams. All with strict instructions to engage no-one, until express permission was granted by Command Central.

Dasha had swallowed her impatience and agreed, thrilled beyond words to be granted leave to come here at all. She had grown even more excited with the readings as they drew closer. There were far more worlds and species landing than she thought possible.

Blue Earth was opening up from the last Terraforming War, and becoming more accessible.

Dasha stared into the red gold flames of the searing fire, and shivered.

Even with the jumps, it was a long way to this planet. It was certainly the longest she had been on a ship. The longest any of them had been on a ship. She could see why the Federation had been content, for the most part, to leave it be.

They had not interceded in the last Terraforming War at all, which was unusual for them. It was rumored the powers that be in the Federation secretly hoped the Old Ones and the Luciienns would blow themselves, and perhaps the planet, to pieces and be done with it.

As it was, what the Luciienns did do, was much cleverer.

The Federation was happy.

They could work with it.

The Federation had always existed in uneasy truce, and often extremely gray area collusion, with the Old Ones. If someone else was able to keep at least some of the Old Ones under control, they would most happily leave them to it.

The beings of Luciienn had done it from the sea.

It was the mystery that would baffle the future inhabitants of Blue Earth for many years. These memories they held deep in their consciousness of these beings from the sea.

The horned ones. The mermaids. The lost city. The songs.

Sailors knew. Because sailors still felt their presence, saw their shadows, heard their song.

And what a song.

It did not come from the sea, but there are many in earth's seas who echo it. Or at least some of it.

It came from Luciienn. Brightest of stars in this corner of the Cosmos. The Light Bringer. The Questioner.

Such lies told about it and the beings who descended from it.

There was only the smallest tribe of star children here when the Luciienns came. Born of star dust and space rocks. Older than this planet and pounding into it from long ago and far away.

The Luciienns walked briefly among them before the first TerraformingWar. Before the first attack of the Old Ones. The star children hid in the caves. The Luciienns dove deep into the seas. It was a smart move. The Old Ones were unaware the Luciienns could live underwater as well as atop of it. The Sirens were flying creatures after all. But in the seas of Blue Earth the Sirens and the Pann Lords expertly adapted their forms.

They made great show of building a city.

But it was always a city meant to be sacrificed.

They let the Old Ones mass on the land above in sufficient numbers.

And then they sacrificed their city and destroyed all of them.

They had saved this Blue World from the Old Ones' intended terraforming.

They had cut off their oxygen. And an Old One's oxygen is power. But they could no longer transition to Blue Earth without losing most of it.

So, the Old Ones stayed off the planet proper, and contented themselves with the Webs they wove around it. But it takes many, many years of an age or more to build the Webs which encircle worlds. And the Old Ones would not have a significant foothold here until a group of their human slavers were forced to flee Red Marza.

And they settled here, and did the Old Ones bidding.

But this was later. Much later.

Which was fortunate, because Dasha of the Federation had enough to deal with in the time she was here, without adding Old Ones to the mix.

Soon after landing she had gotten off the ship and gone walking. It was a thing of hers. She walked constantly. Two Security Detail trailed half-heartedly along behind her. It was protocol, but they were not expecting any trouble. They were only here to observe after all, not to compete for time or prizes from the Godd Mists. And they were the Federation, after all. If there was trouble it would be amongst the riders and the beings around the fires. They had strict orders to observe that only, if it arose, and not intervene.

She had gotten ahead of the guards and emerged into a sudden clearing.

The sight before her took her breath away. And the feelings in the glowing land all around, forced her to steady herself on a tree trunk. She could feel the energy in it rolling. Could feel things moving underneath, above, all around her.

The Siren was on top of the male, wings extended. He had his hands tight around her hips. His groans of pleasure were guttural. The Siren's sounds were the most erotic Dasha had ever heard. They moved in unison together, hot, fast, deep, pounding, hard. And like the land, they were glowing.

There were no readings of Sirens on Blue Earth! If there were, the Federation would have sent a larger Security Detail and a larger anthropological team.

There were not even readings of Nephliim!

And then Dasha realized. This was no Nephliim underneath the Siren, although that would have been miracle and spectacle enough. No, this was even rarer to behold. An Ancient Astronaut. And not just any Ancient Astronaut, a Maker. She could tell from his markings.

And then the Siren peaked, and the whole earth shook with it.

One of the Security Detail grabbed her arm and tried to pull her away, his eyes were dark with desire, but he was keeping control, barely. The other crashed through the bush towards them and pushed clumsily into her. He was most definitely not in control, and unthinking, he ground against her.

The other shouted at him and pushed him back from her.

"Shoosh! Shoosh" Dasha hissed frantically at him, but it was too late. They had caught the attention of the Ancient Astronaut. And slowly he turned his head to them, and fixed them with his eyes as he came.

They could not move. They stood transfixed under that gaze until he was finished.

He looked away from them only long enough to pull the Siren down on top of him and kiss her long and deep.

She stretched languorously and moved off of him quickly. Turning to face the three of them still transfixed on the edge of the clearing, she smiled at them knowingly. The Security Detail fell to their knees at the sight of her. There were many tales of the Siren's exquisite beauty and the affect they had on those around them. Evidently, these tales were not exaggerations.

She was totally unselfconscious and magnificent.

Dasha turned to the Ancient Astronaut still lying on the ground. He was naked still and enormous. Dasha trembled and felt her own knees go out from under her.

He smiled. A small, knowing smile, eerily similar to the Siren's.

The beings dressed slowly and unperturbed in front of them, talking quietly in a tongue unknown to Dasha. Still not one of the three of them could move. They kneeled there as these mighty beings left them, with not a backward glance, the waves of their presence and the aftermath of their sex still rolling through the atmosphere.

Godds! Dasha was suddenly on fire. The men groaned, feeling it also, and this time it was the one who had shown control before who reached for her.

His tongue was down her throat and his hand was on her breast before she even knew what was happening.

Mortified, Dasha pushed him away. The other guard was still kneeling there, staring hungrily at them.

"We need to get to camp and report this immediately," Dasha's voice was hoarse. Quickly, she zipped up her top, still deeply embarrassed.

"Move! Now!" She kicked out at the nearest kneeling man. He looked at her, shocked, but it had the desired effect.

Dasha felt the heat in their eyes on her back all the way back to the ship. She made her report quickly and locked herself in her cabin. Federation Command Central was ecstatic. An Ancient Astronaut, a Maker no less, and a Siren. She must make contact if she saw them again. Try to talk to them.

Dasha nodded her assent while secretly praying there would be no such encounters for any of them. She had been unprepared for anything like that. She did not know how to deal with it.

The next day, the Security Detail were cool and professional with her. Distant.

Dasha did not want to know what they said amongst themselves.

She sat before the campfire and immersed herself in a report of her analysis of the status of the last terraforming attempt on Blue Earth.

She could see from their feeds that the Godd Mists were close. Hopefully they could into full play tomorrow and distract everyone.

Day, night. She could not see any difference between the two, but she could feel them. It was like a form of torture. She had longed to be here, begged to be here. Now, she could not wait to be off this world.

The mystery of night came - for how did she know it was night? - and she was still by the fire, lost in her analysis.

Everyone else was in bed. The bots were standing watch. The campfire crackled. All else was quiet.

She was suddenly very aware of the sound of her tapping on the screen. Suddenly aware of a sweat down her back and hairs lifting up on her neck.

She was chilled in spite of the fire, and suddenly so scared she had an awful feeling she might wet herself.

She looked up and there they were. Two huge Nephliim. They had come to stand across the fire from her.

They folded their arms across their chests and stared.

It was a look of challenge and contempt and other things.

It was not a look anyone wants to see from such beings. Their size and physical power was matched with intellect, magic and aggression. Ancient and giant, and filled with a presence and such knowledge. Ah, such knowledge.

Just the weight of them near was like a shield grip.

Godds, Nephliim here too! What else were they not detecting? *How* were they not detecting! Dasha trembled under their gaze. Was it just these two? Were there more here? Would they fight the Ancient Astronauts? Was the one she'd seen with the Siren the only one?

As she thought the last, one of the Nephliim leaned his face forward over the fire and growled at her.

He was muscled and huge. As big as the Ancient Astronaut, easily. She could see how the famed battles between the two would have been mighty.

But this was no place for her. And there was no reason for this aggression towards her. Was it the approach of the Godd Mists turning them all crazy? Dasha shoved aside all dignity, pressed the alarm on her comms and screamed.

The bots were there in an instant, with blasters.

Dasha had a sudden horrible thought that the Federation would consider her more expendable than the Nephliim.

They had not moved.

The bots activated the hum of red tracers on them.

The Nephliim laughed and moved off slowly into the indigo shadows.

Dasha would not leave the ship the next day.

Federation Command Central contacted her with new orders.

They no longer had any interest in the other worlds and species there, which Dasha had hoped to study. Her orders had changed, they said. She was to concentrate all efforts on the Sirens, the Ancient Astronauts, and the Nephliim.

Still they could not read their presence. It was the thing the Federation was most intrigued about. How such beings - and three different species at that - were cloaking their presence from them so completely. And what exactly they were doing, on Blue Earth? They sent one of the bots a language enhancement in the old tongue. She must converse with them at the first available opportunity.

Well, they could stay intrigued, Dasha thought to herself grimly. Federation orders to converse be damned. The people giving these orders had never been in the presence of these creatures. Never felt the weight and the threat of them upon them.

That night she sat on the flight deck and did her work there.

The ship was secure. Nothing could get to her. The Security Detail had eased a little in her company again, and one of them had stayed up with the bots.

He was a good, solid, silent human presence beside her while she worked. And he had let her keep the shields down in this area.

Dasha stretched and looked at the time. A bathroom break, an hour or so more, and then she was done for the night.

"Bathroom break," she announced.

The Security Detail nodded, "I'm gonna lift the shields, have a quick look."

"Ok," Dasha yawned, feeling more relaxed about it now. It had been there process all night. When she went for a bathroom break, he would take a quick walk outside or just lift the shields.

Command Central did not want the shields down at all. But Command Central could screw itself, Dasha thought as she made her way down the brightly lit corridor. It had all been good so far tonight though. Neither the Security Detail or the Bot had found signs of anyone or anything around them.

The ship's bathrooms were tiny and lit with the most ghastly sick shade of blue, that would make anyone look disgusting. As if there wasn't enough blue on this planet already, Dasha thought wryly to herself, as she washed her hands and tried fervently not to look at her blue reflection. If any Federation ship was going to make this godds-forsaken journey again, she would tell them to put different colored lights in the bathrooms. Red, yellow, hell, even green would have been an improvement.

The corridor she walked down was quiet now with the hum of the emergency lighting. It must have come on while she was in the bathroom.

Dasha stepped out of the corridor and felt a chill of fright when she saw the shields were still up.

The Security Detail was on alert, gun raised. The bots were right outside the ship, blasters pointing out into the night and tracking.

It flashed bright and quick as lightening through the bush to the right of them. Dasha screamed.

"Get back into the corridor!" the Security Detail commanded. He walked backwards, covering them both with his blaster, forcing her back the way she'd come.

But not before she saw them both. The two Nephliim had climbed atop a large rock. They were still below, but they stared up at her as she backed past the last expanse of window.

One of them tapped his head with his finger and then pointed at her, smiling knowingly. The other drew his hand across his throat.

Godds! What did they want from her!

It was too much. The dread overtook her. She felt sick that there would be no daylight to relieve the terror of the night, because there was no day.

In her cabin she shook and rocked herself and would not talk to anyone. The Security Detail wisely called for the med-bot who administered a strong sedative.

It was the only way she would have slept at all. They kept her out like that for a full day.

And when she awoke, they had good news for her.

The Godd Mists had started. And the Nephliims' only interest appeared to only be in them now.

They did not tell her of the small native creature they had found dead outside the ship, atop the rock the Nephliim had stood on. An obsidian shard with Nephliim feathers and gems wedged deep into its skull.

There were runes smeared onto the rock with the creature's blood.

They did not tell her that either. She would not be going outside, and there was no chance she would see it. They all had strict orders to stay on the ship while the Godd Mists were in full play.

And they watched, entranced, all of them, from the flight deck, and via the feeds from the drones, as the Godd Mists toyed with the beings there to ride them. Appearing and disappearing at will, white and gold and silver. The relief of something other than indigo affected them all profoundly.

The Godd Mists allowed those who dared, and were skilled enough, the briefest of rides, before they spat them out, wild eyed and raving.

When the rush and the initial madness subsided, the riders were often quiet for days, lost in a euphoric void between worlds they could only describe as sweet ecstasy.

Some not few died in those mists.

And some seemed never to return from the void.

The ones that came out the other side were changed. Permanently.

Through the feeds from the drones, Dasha only saw one come through and declare he was out. The rest simply gathered their strength around the fires and plotted to ride again. And always there was talk of crystals in the mists and wagers on who would claim them.

Dasha was familiar with the crystals they coveted. She had been briefed on them before coming here, and she had studied the one the Federation had in its possession. Obtained by a rider of eons ago. But there was a different crystal rumored in these mists, and the Federation had expressed a passing interest in that one, should any come out with it.

They had not seemed to place too much importance on it, and so neither had Dasha. But now that she was here, it was evident this was what many were riding for.

But there were none who came out with any crystals at all, that they saw, let alone this one that consumed them. And the Godd Mists began to wane and temper.

Their orders came to go outside.

"Are you Ok?" It was the Security Detail looking at her concernedly.

"Yes," she breathed, and then more certainly, "Yes." But her voice shook and her eyes were a little wild.

"Shoot to kill," the Security Detail said. They had given her a gun. "I'll be right beside you."

"Thank you," she whispered, remembering his kiss and his hand on her breast, and wishing it had happened under different circumstances.

He clasped her shoulder firmly and smiled kindly at her.

They walked outside.

And the Elementals came.

And none of them, not even the Nephliim were prepared for them.

They were beyond terror.

They were mist also.

And they were indigo.

But chameleon too, in that they would suddenly take on other colors in the air. Mostly when they killed, and mostly the colors of death. Of blood and organs and muscle. And they were madness far beyond anything they had already witnessed on this world.

They roared through this world of indigo and fire and Godd Mists and mythic beings. Their purpose and motivations indiscernible to any but themselves.

They were under heavy attack. She could hear someone yelling at her, "Hold your space! Hold your space! Hold your space!"

Crack!

The bush three foot to her right lit up with a blue fire, and Dasha dove to her left as the huge winged body of the Terradactyl fell charred and smoking where she had just been crouching.

The smell of sulphur and burning flesh made her retch. A charging King Saur crashed through the bushes to her right. He was huge. He could reach down with his great head and eat her in three bites. Their eyes made brief contact. The blood lust filling his, and the paralyzed fear filling Dasha's.

The Security Detail pushed in front of her, sheltering her body, his blaster pointed at the huge creature.

And then an Elemental was upon them all, man, woman and Saur. And the weight of it brought them to their knees, gasping.

It was so heavy.

And yet there was nothing to fight against.

It was mist.

But it felt like an army had descended upon them.

Dasha couldn't breathe. Her heart beat fit to burst. The hairs on her body stood up and she dripped in cold sweat. She had never felt such power. Such power, crushing her, exploring her pushing its way into her like she was as inconsequential as air.

And then it howled.

And the sound split the air in two.

She screamed like she had never screamed before.

And it was like it rode her terror. And it rode her from the inside out.

It rode her terror and it fed her terror. And her terror grew. It became physical.

It was excruciating.

Her skin started to tear and bleed. And Dasha cried. She curled into a ball and sobbed. Lost in a terror that was so great and so engulfing she thought her heart would surely stop then and there.

She felt the pressure on her skull and knew the end was near.

And then she felt its hesitation.

It sniffed at her like a dog.

She heard the battle cries of the Nephliim closing in on them.

The Elemental howled.

It slashed at her head, opening a deep red gouge along the back of her crown.

Dasha shrieked in agony.

A laser from the weapons of the Nephliim whizzed over her, and exploded into the Elemental.

It flinched. For just a mili-second it flinched.

And then it was off.

Whirling through the bush and leaving blue fire in its wake.

And one of the Nephliim from across the fire stood over her. His face was mask like, unreadable.

She stayed curled in a ball, shivering violently.

She closed her eyes.

She felt him bend down.

Felt his fingers in the red gouge and knew fresh agony.

Heard him place something on the ground beside her.

She passed out from pain and terror in equal measure.

Much time later, when she came to, she saw it was a weapon.

Dasha staggered to her feet. The King Saur was dead and stinking beside her. And, "No!" She felt tears smart in her eyes. The Security Detail was crushed underneath the

Saur. His eyes were open and his hand was outstretched towards her. He had died reaching for her.

Sobbing, Dasha closed his eyes and picked up the Nephliim weapon.

It was big and heavy on her.

Still, it comforted her. She used it constantly at first. Turning and firing it on the slightest of sounds.

The gouge in her head bled constantly and left her woozy. She tore a strip from the shirt of a dead rider and bound her head tight with it.

She could not find the ship and she had no idea how long she wandered lost and talking to herself in the bush.

She stopped talking only when she ran out of water and her lips blistered and her tongue swelled.

But the chatter in her mind was constant.

It spoke of a mind crystal, a mind diamond.

It meant nothing to her.

She lay down and lost consciousness.

She was barely aware of the trickle at first.

Only that her sore head rested comfortably in a lap. A voice in a language she did not understand murmured something. And the very air tingled with electricity at these murmurings. Like the very air was excited to hear them.

And as the voice murmured, she began to understand more of the mind crystal.

And when her understanding was almost complete, she realized that the trickle was water being gently given to her.

She opened her mouth hungrily and lapped at it greedily.

"Easy," the beautiful voice spoke to her in her own language.

Dasha's green eyes flashed open and were met by a pair of violet ones, flecked with gold and framed by long, dark lashes.

Tiny dark golden horns protruded from a wealth of hair. Black wings, also flecked with the same deep golden rose up around the being, protecting Dasha from the elements, sheltering them both.

The golden flecks were the same as the flame, Dasha thought absently to herself.

The creature gently shifted Dasha's head from her lap and laid it on the earth.

"Thank you for bringing the crystal," the Siren said to her, as she rose gracefully.

As the sound of her great wings faded, the hum of the small rescue ship replaced them.

"Siren of Luciienn," Dasha muttered to herself. "What am I?" she called hoarsely after the Siren, suddenly realizing. "What am I?" she yelled more forcefully and coughed madly. But the Siren was long gone.

"How did it get in my head?" she wailed as they placed her on a stretcher and took her aboard the ship. "How did it get in my head!" she demanded. She was hysterical.

"How did what get in your head?" the medic said kindly as he prepared a sedative.

"The crystal. It was in my head all along." Her eyes were wild and she gripped his arm tightly. "He took it. He took it out. It wasn't in them! It wasn't in the Godd Mists! It was in me!"

A man she'd never seen before with strange glittery eyes, stayed the medic's hand and leaned towards her.

"Who took the crystal, my dear?"

"The Nephliim," she said, and then quietened. "You are not the Federation."

"No, not quite, my dear." The man gestured to the medic, who quickly administered the sedative.

At least Dasha, crystal bearer, thought it was a sedative, and she closed her eyes in relief, and let the chemicals take her.

They took her to a peaceful place. A quiet place.

There were many colors.

And there was no indigo.

It was an Old Ones sleep. A forgetting sleep.

She should have fought it with every ounce of strength left in her.

But there was no ounce, and they had taken her by surprise and unknowing of them.

The way the man with the glittery eyes tore her head apart with his hands was horrible.

He found nothing. The Nephliim had been thorough.

The Old One cursed and kicked Dasha's body from the ship in disgust.

She landed on a space rock, freshly jutting clear of Blue Earth's surface after the recent Godd Mists. A Federation Security Detail lay near it under the body of a Saur. When he had eyes, he had used them extensively to look after the well-being of Dasha, crystal bearer. He thought she was the most beautiful, intelligent woman he had ever known. He had no eyes now. They had been pecked out by scavengers. And his spirit had long left this place for the Cosmos beyond.

As the jutting space rock pierced her heart and Dasha dematerialized to dust, his spirit was aware of a deep loss, and he reached out to her, as he had reached out to her, all the time he had known her.

But Dasha, crystal bearer, still deep in the sleep of the Old Ones, remained none the wiser.

Left Behind

The sunlight dapples green through the leafy canopy. My window is never closed. Not when the wind howls, or the rain comes down in sheets. They left us here. But that is Ok. I am queen here. queen of my own rota. Which is not really mine, but better than theirs, and more mine than not.

There is just one sun here, and I rise with it. It is too hot in the afternoon to do much of anything, and I laze.

There is one moon, too, and I rise again with it. I love the moon's creatures. Their bright eyes and elegant nocturnal ways enchant me long into the night. Eventually I sleep light and dream deep, secure in her watch, until the rays of the other rouse me from my wanderings.

My rota. My world.

Some nights I don't sleep at all. And those are the special nights. The nights for my little part in the great rituals I learned before, far, far away from here. But I don't talk about them anymore because once they got me into trouble.

So now I keep them to myself. I hug them secretly to me. My secrets in the sleepless nights. After them, I am more rested, more exhilarated than any sleep could bring. But we don't talk of them. No. No, we don't.

He may come today. I know nothing anymore of days of this strange calendar, but I can sense his coming always.

His rota must be strange to include me in it still.

Perhaps not strange. There is nothing strange about him. Generous.

The cassowaries won't come near today. They can sense his coming as well as I. Mathilda will bark a little. But she will stay close as always.

I chuckle. It would take more than mere man to occasion her retreat. She caught a small bird from a ground nest last time he was here. Vain thing, showing off in front of him. Or perhaps she was just hungry. Quick we are to attribute our emotions to creatures innocent of such things.

Innocent. I ponder this as I see her scuttle suddenly away from where she had carefully camouflaged herself so I had no knowledge of her. She does not look innocent. A terrifying thing really. Eight legs, eight eyes, and of a monstrous size.

I wonder, sometimes, what thoughts go on behind those eyes. Are there any? And even if they were revealed to us, would we recognize them?

Watchers, my friend used to say. Dropped from the Motherships to keep a close eye on us and report back our business.

Is that what you do Mathilda? Report back my business to those who left us here?

If you do, then tell them this.

Their worlds are nothing to me now.

I will not think of them.

I will not give them acknowledgement.

I will not wait for them to return.

I may be an experiment. But I will not be a willing one.

This world I stand upon, is everything to me now. My reality. My world. My rota.

I finish my breakfast and head for the creek. I swim. I return and wash my hair in the old bush shower I rigged myself so very long ago. In a patch of sunlight, I breathe.

I dress. In flowing things. My rings, my beads. I like to appear queen here. An exotic, fragrant, thing. I burn my incense and anoint myself with the oils he brought me last time.

My hair is dry already. It is very hot today. I listen.

As the sounds engulf me, I paint, I write, I clap, I sing. The music of my world pours into the colors on the bark, the canvas, the page, the drum.

The feeling passes. I am suddenly very tired. I retreat.

His gentle voice arouses me from slumber. My eyes open on to the face of love. Crinkled eyes, weathered storms, sorrow, laughter, fear, compassion, laughter, legacy. He will leave one. I will leave one too. We will both leave one. So very, very different, one to the other. And yet here we are, all the same.

I smile, extend my hand. He helps me rise and holds me close. The warmth of his embrace pure joy. Pure giving, without thought of receipt in any way.

He pulls away to look at me. His queen. Queen of the Forest. Queen of my own rota.

There are no inane pleasantries. No meaningless, hand me down rote words of greeting, which are no greeting at all, when it comes down to it.

There are eyes and touch.

And when there is enough of both of those, I move away to make us something to drink while he unpacks what he has brought me.

"I've brought your paints. I couldn't get the magenta. But it's on order and they should have it in two weeks or so. Ah…."

He stops, the air in the room charges with something other, and I turn to him expectantly.

"You might have to wait longer for it though. I won't be back in these parts for a little while."

My head swims, my heart contracts, and I miss him unbearably already. Though I knew this day would come, I am unprepared.

"Oh, don't you cry now!" He smiles compassionately at me, as he wipes away one tell-tale tear with his well-worn thumb. "I'll be back in six weeks or so."

I sniffle and nod and try desperately to believe my own lies. "Oh, don't mind me. I'm a silly old fool who would cry at anything. Don't mind me. Here, drink this, before it gets cold."

All through the night, through our modest dinner and grand conversation, I eat him up with my eyes. I savor him. Every sweet inch of him is committed forever to the biggest swell of my heart and the grandest room of my memories.

I would rip my own heart from my chest and gift it to him.

But he would not accept it. He is tired.

"It's a long, hard walk to your castle, princess," he murmurs. As he eases himself back on the bed beneath my window.

"Queen," I remind him gently, and kiss each eyelid gently closed. As he sleeps, I hold his hand, and weep silent and convulsive beside his dreams.

He stays another night, and we make love beneath my window. He explained it all to me once. How it lets me out, as much as it lets all else in.

And then he is gone again. Laden with my potions and charms, which I heap upon him, as if mere I could change the fate he has chosen for himself.

Mathilda barks softly at his parting.

As he leaves, I notice one of the cassowaries, walks quiet and peaceful by his side. In a patch of sunlight, I breathe, but I am unprepared. I weep.

I swim, walk, eat, sleep, talk to my creatures, my friends. I walk more. I create. I make an Urn. I spend hours at my potting wheel, working elegant shapes between my hands. I cannot drum. I cannot sing. But the creatures and the forest sing. Their singing is a constant thing. And that is good enough for me right now.

The season makes way for the next. The rain comes down in sheets. The earth reeks with a heady richness. Everything is green. Green with a jewel like intensity. A new creature, a new friend. And he is green too. He serenades me with frog like devotion, and falteringly at first, I serenade him back. I can sing once more.

Dry. I sit on my rickety, makeshift steps and sip my tea. The heat pierces my body in wave after wave after wave. I have no paints. I have no manufactured food. I must venture in to town soon. If he doesn't come.

He doesn't come. And so, I venture. It has been a long time since I made this journey. As I follow the small track, I see it through his eyes, and I imagine his thoughts. I am unprepared. I retreat.

On my third attempt, I make it the whole way in. I even remember to bring some of my potting and my smaller paintings. I sell them to Eva for her craft stall. Eva is like me. Left here. My vintage. My world. She always buys my potting and my paintings. Always makes sure I am alright. We do not age like this where we come from. Do they laugh? The ones that left us here, to see us thus?

Eva used to come and visit me in my castle too. But no more.

"It's a long, hard walk to your castle, Kyrridwen," she says now.

"That's what he says too," I muse.

"Have you heard?" she asks gently.

I begin to shake.

I begin to shake violently.

Gently, gently, she leads me to a chair. A cup of sweet tea in my hands. The tears pour freely down her cheeks as she tells me. But they are no match for the floodgates which open in my old white head. I wail senseless for hours.

Eva says to stay here. She says I look tired. "Are you prepared?" she asks quietly.

I shake my head. "No," I whisper. But I can't stay here. I can't breathe here. Eva packs some food for me. She packs my Magenta paint.

It came in eight weeks ago. Has it been that long? That long since his passing?

Yes. He went to the medics in the capital, and they cut him and tried to cut it. But in the end, its cut was the deepest.

"He had the most beautiful funeral," Eva sniffed. "People came from all around."

I didn't come though, did I. Because I didn't know. That is the price of being queen here. Queen of the forest. Queen of my own rota.

I could have taught him how to heal here. Taught him the magic of his soul, and the magic of this world.

No cutting. No cutting. No cutting.

But that was not his way. And his own path, and the gifts he gave to the world, were as sweet and true, as the chosen manifesto of any of us.

I have one of my secret little night rituals in honor of him. I bury him in a way I deem fitting. If he's watching he would have liked it. But he would have liked his town funeral better. I know it. And that is just the way it is. We were different, he and I. What we had in common was beyond mere hobbies.

I make the trip into town more often now. Not to sell my painting, or my potting, or see Eva, or buy food.

People came.

They made Eva give up the market stall. They took her away to the capital. Perhaps they would have tried to take me to. Perhaps they couldn't find me.

But no matter, I find I don't eat much anymore. No, now when I come in, it is just to lay beautiful, jewel green leaves on his grave.

I finished my Urn. I painted it magenta. A big green frog lives in it. Mathilda still barks. Still spies on me and reports back to the Motherships. The cassowaries still visit. I sleep, I paint, I sing, I clap, I dance, I dream.

We have walked among you for so long now, on your beautiful world.

Can you not tell?

Can you not feel us?

No matter.

They are coming for me.

They are coming for us all.

I am unprepared.

But I find a patch of sunlight.

And I breathe, I breath, I breathe.

*****

Thank you!

Thank you so much for reading Off-Worlders. I'm honored to share this collection of stories with you. If you would be so kind as to share a review at your place of purchase, it would be very much appreciated. The small act of leaving a review - no matter how short - helps make what Authors like myself do, possible.

For new release info and the occasional musing, please join my mailing list at:

www.sarahsofiadelaunay.com

www.ingramcontent.com/pod-product-compliance
Lightning Source LLC
Chambersburg PA
CBHW021034130626
46552CB00005B/1830